THE SPIKED BOY

Dick Palmer and Will Snell are great friends, both former highwaymen who were subsequently exonerated. However, they become fugitives from the law again when members of a mysterious gang of murderers and kidnappers use their names to frame them. Then when the gang kidnap Palmer's wife the two friends are plunged into a deadly struggle to rescue her. But they are up against an evil and secret organization — and the sadistic Simon Pendexter, who swings a 'spiked boy' . . .

JOHN RUSSELL FEARN

◆

THE
SPIKED BOY

Complete and Unabridged

LINFORD
Leicester

First published in Great Britain

First Linford Edition
published 2009

British Library CIP Data

Fearn, John Russell, *1908 – 1960*
  The spiked boy
  1. Historical fiction.
  2. Large type books.
  I. Title
  823.9'12–dc22

  ISBN 978–1–84782–637–4

Published by
F. A. Thorpe (Publishing)
Anstey, Leicestershire

Set by Words & Graphics Ltd.
Anstey, Leicestershire
Printed and bound in Great Britain by
T. J. International Ltd., Padstow, Cornwall

This book is printed on acid-free paper

1

Out of the City of London and down Ludgate Hill thundered a single horseman. Great was his speed as he galloped towards Lincoln Inn Fields. Suddenly there appeared a pursuing troop of horsemen some distance behind.

He was a giant of a fellow with a fine red beard and riding a great black stallion that frothed at the mouth and strained at the reins in a truly frightening manner. The bearded giant glanced swiftly behind at the troop of horsemen and then spurred his horse to greater efforts, and the stallion, no whit abashed, charged along at an even greater pace

The troop of horsemen seemed unconcerned and was moving at an easy canter down the hill. Yet still the bearded man rode hell for leather. He was well armed; his pockets bulged with any number of pistols and the handle of a large sailor's knife protruded from his belt.

Ahead of the lone rider, perhaps a mile distant, lay a white, gabled house with a sweeping drive before it. The sun glittered down upon a pleasant scene — a slim, young man strolled languidly on the lawn before his home, and at his side there tripped a pretty damsel with beautiful black tresses curled upon her bare shoulders. He was neatly dressed in black in the latest mode for the eighteenth century and was in earnest conversation, discussing some new business venture. She clung to his arm and listened quietly, and now and then glanced up at her companion as he raised his voice to emphasise some point or other.

Upon this peaceful, law-abiding scene the aforementioned wicked-looking horseman suddenly appeared, careering up the drive and coming to a halt with much snorting, slithering and bellowing as his reins were pulled abruptly.

The young man frowned, pushed his wife behind him, drew a pistol and cocked it in one swift movement. Then, as the rider dismounted, his mouth fell agape and almost immediately he leaped forward, crying out in delight:

'Will Snell!'

An expansive grin spread across the giant's flushed face. 'Yes, it's me, Dick, an' how are you?'

'Why, fine Will — fine, but what brings you in such a hurry?'

'Ah, we have not much time, Dick, but first I must pay my respects to Jeanette.' And with this he smiled at the girl by the young man's side, bowed over her extended hand and kissed it gently. For all his bulk he carried out this gracious movement surprisingly well.

'It is a pleasure to see you again, Will,' she said.

Will Snell bowed again and then turned quickly back to Dick Palmer. 'Dick,' he exclaimed in his powerful voice, 'I am afraid I bring had tidings.'

At once the couple looked anxious and waited for his next words.

'There is not time now for a lengthy explanation — I can tell you in full when we are on the move — but some rogues out in Surrey and Sussex are using our names on the high road and some peace

3

officers are out seeking us — this very moment they are on the road here from London.'

Dick Palmer frowned. 'Using our names, but why?'

'That I don't know — the fact remains they are,' Will Snell replied, glancing at Jeanette, 'and I am afraid we must fly this instant.'

Dick Palmer muttered beneath his breath, for he realised he had to make a quick decision. At last he turned to his wife and kissed her upon the forehead. 'Fear not, my dear, we will clear up this matter in no time at all and then I shall return.' He faced Will Snell again. 'How far distant are these officers?'

'Not a mile.'

Palmer squeezed his wife's arm. 'There is no alternative, Jeanette, as Will says, we must fly. I will call Nick and tell him to saddle Red Ruby and change into my riding clothes.' With this he hurried into the house, leaving Jeanette standing forlornly at the side of the great Will Snell.

Soon there was a pattering of feet as

Nicholas Wilken hurried to the stables at the back of the house. Then there was silence for a moment or two. This was followed by the footsteps of Palmer as he reappeared in black riding dress and the clip-clop of a horse's hoofs along the side of the house. In a moment young Nicholas Wilken came into view leading a magnificent chestnut mare with a fine, russet coloured mane.

'Aha, so you still have that beautiful beast,' cried Will, gazing admiringly at the slim, powerful lines of the mare.

Palmer nodded and, without more ado, whilst the boy held the bridle, he swung into the saddle. Will immediately did likewise and they were ready.

Dick smiled down reassuringly at his wife. 'Do not worry, my dear, nothing will stop me from returning, and that as soon as this foolish matter is settled.'

She smiled back at him, reassured a little, and waved her arm. Palmer raised his hand in salute, as did Will Snell, and then they both swung their horses about and galloped off down the drive. At the gate Will pointed in the opposite direction to the road to London and they thundered up to the nearby brow of a hill. Here Palmer slowed down slightly, turned in the saddle and waved again to the little figure on the lawn in front of the white house, then, with compressed lips, he spurred after Will Snell and raced down the far side of the hill.

The two galloped along over the rough road, past scattered cottages and between high hedgerows, speaking not, for at the moment they needed to put as many miles as possible between themselves and the troop of peace officers. Having travelled thus for some time, Will Snell at last reduced his speed.

'I have in mind an inn near Byfleet in Surrey we can stay for tonight,' he roared to Palmer. 'It is on the edge of the strange activities of which I'll tell you in a few moments.'

Dick Palmer nodded and they galloped on again. In a little while they came to an old wooden bridge spanning the River Thames, and around about there clustered a few cottages. Here there was a tollgate and a large, aggressive looking man appeared from a hut at the side.

'Fourpence,' he bellowed.

Will gave a grunt, but handed over the coins and thereupon the spiked gate was swung open. Digging in their spurs the two friends were off again, and now the road was smoother and they made good progress. Shortly they entered a small wood and when halfway through Will held up one large hand and reined in his steed.

'Let's find a glade,' he cried, 'it will be safest off the high road and then I can tell you of the events that have been taking place in Surrey — it's a most strange affair.' With that he led the way off the road and into the trees. They threaded their way for some distance before abruptly coming out into a tiny green dell surrounded by bushes and trees. The sun glanced down through the branches giving the place a pleasant, bespeckled appearance, and the air was filled with the song of birds.

Will Snell threw himself down upon the bank with a tired sigh. Dick seated himself nearby and stared somewhat sadly up at the blue sky. Will glanced at his young friend and grinned broadly.

'It will not be long before you see her again Dick — cheer up.'

Palmer smiled. 'Yes — that's true, Will. Come now, tell me this story — you have got me all curious.'

Leaning back and clasping his great hands behind his head Will Snell then recounted this adventure. 'I was returning from Portsmouth,' he said, 'at which place I had done a little business.' At Palmer's sly grin, the giant looked offended. 'No, no Dick — believe it or not, it was honest business!'

'I apologise Will,' said Palmer solemnly. 'Carry on.'

'As I say, I was returning from Portsmouth and I had reached a little place called Nobham, which is near Byfleet in Surrey. I was in a joyous mood for my trip to Portsmouth had proved most profitable — which reminds me Dick,' added Will glancing at his friend, 'did you bring any money?'

'Yes I did — I thought of that.'

'Good. Well, as I rode into Nobham

— feeling as I say mighty cheerful — I noticed the village blacksmith sitting outside his smithy looking most downcast.

'"Ahoy,' I says to him, 'what ails you on such a pleasant day?'

'He looked up and the sight of his face gave me a shock, for his eyes were red-rimmed as if he had been crying, and altogether he looked most sorrowful. Feeling pity for the fellow — me being in such high spirits — I drew in my horse and dismounted in front of him.

'He stared up at me from his bloodshot eyes for some time, and I could see he was debating whether to unfold his troubles to me or not. At all events he must ha' taken to me because he says:

'"It's me daughter.'

'"Your daughter?' says I, 'and what is wrong with the damsel?'

'"She's taken,' says he, glancing at me doubtfully as if still not sure he should tell me.

'"Taken,' says I — as you will appreciate, Dick,' Will remarked, interrupting himself, 'I had to drag his tale out of him piece by piece.'

''Yes — and I don't know where.'

'I sat down on the bench by his side, holding my steed in front of me. 'Come now,' I cried, 'who has taken her and why?'

''She's kidnapped,' he wailed.

''Yes, yes — but who has done this vile deed?'

'He looked at me strangely. 'Have you not heard? Hereabouts we are terrorised by a gang of thieves, highwaymen and footpads.'

'At this I looked surprised, for it was news to me. 'Is it now?' I cried, 'and it's they that have taken her?'

''Yes,' and thereupon he threw his hands in the air in a hopeless fashion and then his head fell forward upon his chest, and he gazed dismally at my horse's shoes.

''Hasn't the sheriff of this county taken the matter in hand?' I asked.

''He has, but to little avail. There is a troop of catchpolls in the neighbourhood, but these rogues they seek just disappear.'

'I can tell you, Dick,' said Will

seriously, 'I could see that here was no normal matter, as you will find if you can but bear me a little longer.'

'I find the story greatly interesting, Will — pray continue.'

' 'Have they no proof?' I asked him.

' 'Very little,' grunted the blacksmith (whose name I found out to be Tom Broughton).

' 'Don't they know anything at all?'

' 'No, 'cept the names of two of 'em — and these fellows be right brave, for they brag their names wherever they go.'

' 'Do they — and what are their names?'

'Now, Dick,' said Will Snell, sitting up and lowering his voice, 'as you can well imagine his answer to my question, when you hear it, startled me no end.'

Dick Palmer leaned closer to his friend, now fully taken with Will's story.

' 'Their names?' the blacksmith roared, 'Ha, I mind them well — one was Dick Palmer and t'other Will Snell!'

'At this I leaps to my feet and glares down at him. 'What, cried I, 'are you sure of this?'

'The blacksmith looked surprised. 'Course I am,' he grunted.

'There was no doubt about it, Dick, the fellow was telling the truth, that I could see. I had to think this news over carefully, so I asked him: 'Is there an inn hereabouts friend, where I might put up for the night?'

' 'Yes,' he nodded, 'the Grasshopper just around yonder corner — 'bout a hundred paces forward.'

' 'Thank you,' I cried, 'farewell,' and I thereupon mounted my steed.

' 'Farewell pal,' he replied.

'With that I spurred forward and rounding the bend at the end of the village beheld, set back a little from the Highway, 'The Grasshopper'. It is a neat, cosy little inn, Dick, nestling beneath great beech trees, and the fare is excellent — you will like the place. My horse was taken from me and tucked away in a little stable at the back. Then I went in and met mine host, the landlord, and his buxom daughter, Mary.

'It was the girl who served me with a most excellent repast, and thereafter, as it was still early evening, I settled down in a corner with my briar and some ale, and took to thinking upon the story told me by the blacksmith.

'The evening passed peacefully and I was just thinking of turning in — Mary was cleaning up behind the bar — when there came the sound of shuffling footsteps outside the door. It was swung open wide from an abrupt push and there staggered in a sight which I hope I shall never see again.'

Will paused to note the reaction upon his young friend, and seeing Dick's wide-open eyes, he continued. 'Mary promptly screamed, which brought the landlord, Alfred Lackton, running from the back of the inn. The man that reeled into the room was, I realised, after I had stared at him some time, Tom Broughton, the blacksmith. I leaped to my feet and, with the landlord, rushed over to him as he crashed to the floor and rolled over on his back.

'Now Dick, I am not at all squeamish as you well know, but the sight of this poor fellow's face fair turned my stomach over. There were great, deep gashes all over as if by some animal's huge claws, or maybe by some kind of spikes, and one side of his face was properly bashed in — blood was everywhere.

'The landlord and I bent over him and the poor devil, seeing me, croaked: 'Ah, my pal, my friend, I must tell you,' and as he spoke blood gushed like a fountain from his torn mouth. 'I must tell you,' he repeated in a feebler voice and I leaned closer. 'They have taken her — they have taken her to — to Toby Joy!' There was a further spurt of blood and his mouth quivered and closed and he lay rigid, his eyes wide open and staring. I knew him to be dead.'

Dick Palmer gave out a long gasp. 'Nay, Will, but you make me shiver.'

'Yes, I can quite understand. I rode off next morning, the landlord saying he would see to the blacksmith's burial and the telling of the affair to the sheriff. He also told me the peace officers were searching for two of the men because they knew their names. I made all speed, following this, to London and it was there, only three days later, that I heard of these officers setting out to collect your good self. And in their possession they carried a general warrant for our arrest!'

2

Dick Palmer stared down at his feet for some time after Will had finished his story. In the meantime the sun sank low in the west so that now there were only streaks of bright light spanning the glade. A hush settled upon the wood, as if the birds and the beasts respected Palmer's desire for peaceful thought.

Will Snell did not, however. Tugging impatiently at his red beard he watched his young friend for several moments and then at last cried:

'Well, Dick. You're the brainy one — what's your opinion of the affair?'

Palmer scratched his fair hair and replied: 'Why, it's undoubtedly a most unpleasant do, Will, but you are as wise as me as to what it all means. The main thing that I can see is that we shall have to tread very delicately — what with the peace officers after us and apparently this gang of rogues — very delicately indeed.'

'Ha, you are right, Dick — we will have to be mighty secretive and cunning.'

'I wonder what this Toby-Joy is,' Dick mused.

'There you have me,' grunted Will. ' "They have taken her to Toby-Joy," he said. And those were his last words.' Will yawned and stretched his great limbs and then suddenly jumped to his feet. 'Come, Dick,' he cried, 'let us continue the journey, else we shall not arrive until after dark.'

They untied their steeds from the nearby tree, were soon in the saddle and winding their way back to the high road. Having made sure there was no one in sight they turned west and broke into a fast canter.

Soon they came to the village of King's Stone and here they increased their speed for there might be peace officers abroad. But whether or not made no difference, for here they must needs cross the River Thames again, and here was another tollgate. Duly paying the charge, and at the same time keeping a wary eye on the road and the green fields about them,

Dick and Will spurred forward again, crossed the high stone bridge, and galloped onward to the village of Nobham.

They now entered heavily wooded country, broken now and then by stretches of enclosed fields with a farm or two and cottages dotted about. As they cantered through a particularly thick wood Will remarked to his friend: 'We must take care on these straight bits of road, else we might be caught.' Scarce were his words uttered than the two men turned a corner and beheld, some three hundred paces ahead, four horsemen travelling towards them.

'Quick,' snapped Will Snell, 'into the wood,' and he dug in his spurs and shot into the darkness beneath the trees, with Palmer close behind. They rode in some distance and then dismounted and tethered their steeds to a branch. Creeping back to within a few paces of the edge of the wood, they waited for the oncoming horsemen.

'It's doubtful they noticed us in the dusk,' murmured Dick.

'Yes, I only hope you are right, for I fancy not to be taken at this early stage of the game.'

They could now hear the clipperty-clop of the four horses and then the newcomers were abreast the two hidden in the wood. It was still early evening and the four riders could be seen quite clearly. They were big, grim solemn fellows dressed all in black, and they reminded Dick Palmer of a funeral procession, for they moved slowly. The strangers spoke not to one another as they rode, nor even looked upon their companions. Within a minute they were gone upon their doleful way.

Will Snell gave a heavy grunt. 'They're catchpolls with little doubt.'

'Cheerful fellows,' Dick remarked. 'Yes — they are always like that, it's their profession I am sure — a thankless task.'

With these comments they returned to their horses mounted and galloped off along the road. Within an hour they reached the brow of a hill and below, not fifty paces away, lights gleamed from out of the darkness.

'That's Nobham,' announced Will, 'and that first light — 'The Grasshopper'.'

'Good,' grunted Palmer, 'I am both hungry and thirsty.'

'Come then, and let us be fussed over by Mary Lackton.'

They rode down the hill and dismounted before the inn. A lanky youth wandered up to them, said: ' 'Evenin',' took their horses and wandered away again behind the inn. 'The Grasshopper' was a grey, square little place set beneath great trees that spread out over its roof in a protective fashion. Looking at the creaking sign board, Palmer for some time tried to make out the strange painting thereon, then he realised that it was a grasshopper, though to be sure it looked more like a large fish.

Will Snell had already entered the inn and, by the sound of the excited voices within, was being received with some warmth. Palmer followed and stood hesitantly upon the threshold of the cosy, timbered little bar, with its big fireplace and crackling wood fire

'Ha,' roared Will, 'an' this is my great

friend Arthur Snooch, and he waved Dick forward to a dark, short man, and a buxom fair wench. As Dick approached Will whispered: 'My name is George.'

Palmer shook hands with the landlord and his daughter, the latter giving Dick a most coquettish look, which, if the truth be known, pleased him no end.

'Sit down then,' cried the landlord, showing them to a table in an alcove by the fire, 'and let Mary prove what a good cook she is.'

Alfred Lackton went and fetched two brimming tankards full of ale. Will waved him to a stool at the table and when the landlord was seated, said: 'What about the blacksmith, Tom Broughton?'

A look of fear crossed the face of the little man and, having glanced about the bar as if to make sure they were alone, he replied: 'The peace officers came and asked many questions, then they left and I've heard no more — no more I've 'eard.'

Will Snell leaned over close to him and whispered: 'You remember what he said — his dying words?'

'Yes, to be sure I do — not likely am I to forget — nay, I won't forget.'

'Then you have heard no more of this Toby-Joy?'

Alfred Lackton suddenly became very frightened, muttered something about 'seeing you later,' and then scrambled to his feet and hurried away behind the bar.

Will Snell glanced at Dick expressively, but the matter was dropped for the time being, for Mary bounced in carrying two plates piled high with a great repast that gave off a most appetising aroma.

'There you are,' cried she, smiling all over her pink countenance, 'two handsome meals for two handsome men.'

'And served by a very handsome woman,' completed Will, giving a clap of his hands as he espied the great pieces of beef roasted in the midst of a fine variety of vegetables. This bountiful fare was followed by large chunks of cheese and bread, and all the time the landlord's daughter hovered around them watching anxiously for any signs of distaste. But there were no signs and all she could see were two bowed heads, and all she could hear was the sound of masticating jaws.

At last they were finished and they sat back and slapped their lips and smiled appreciatively at Mary. 'Have you had your fill?' asked she, mighty concerned.

'Nay, woman,' replied Dick, patting his stomach. 'I defy any man to still require sustenance after such helpings.

The two lay back, quaffed their ale and remained still and quiet, gazing into the flickering flames of the fire as one does after a large and satisfying meal. Mary Lackton cleared away the remains and tripped off to the rear of the inn, self-consciously patting her fair curls, which bounced up and down on her shoulders as she went.

Dick Palmer and Will Snell appeared a rather strange pair as they lay sprawled in the high-backed wall seat. Dick slim and fair in his smart black coat and waistcoat, breeches and riding boots, and Will large and aggressive with his wild red hair, great muscles bulging beneath his brown coat and leather jerkin. His nickname of Wild Will was most fitting.

The peace of the old bar room was

abruptly broken by a loud snore. Dick and Will sat forward with a jolt and stared hard at the far corner in amazement. This corner of the room was almost in darkness for the lanterns were set at the bar and about the fireplace. But they could now see, protruding from the darkness, a pair of neatly booted feet.

'We are not alone,' gasped Will, and at once got to his feet and strode across the room. Dick Palmer followed and they stared down at a small, tidily dressed man with a great, bulging head. His mouth was wide open and again there issued there from a long, contented snore.

'He's a mighty heavy sleeper,' murmured Palmer.

At that moment Alfred Lackton entered the bar. Will waved him over. 'Who might this be?' he asked.

'Oh, 'im,' said the landlord, looking relieved, 'that's Nodding Ned — he often stops the night 'ere. As you see, 'e be always sleeping.'

The three men gazed curiously down upon the little fellow with the top-heavy head who slept so peacefully.

'Has he been there all time?' asked Dick of the landlord.

'Yes, 'e's been 'ere all h'evenin' — all h'evenin' 'e's been 'ere.'

'Blow me over,' muttered Will. 'Seeing 'im reminds me of something.'

'What's that?' asked Palmer.

'I'm sleepy myself!'

Dick nodded. 'Yes, so am I — come let us away to our beds — where are they landlord?'

'Up the stairs, second door on your right — on your right second door along.'

'Thank you,' grunted Will, and the two friends made their way to the stairs in the corner at one side of the bar. Here Will stopped and turned about: 'Will we be seeing you er — later?' he asked the landlord quietly.

Alfred Lackton momentarily looked nervous and then he jerked his head up and down energetically, and with that rushed off to the back of the inn. Will and Dick climbed the stairs and reached their room — a small but cosy place with a tiny window overlooking the stable yard.

'He is a mighty frightened cove,'

grunted Will, throwing off his boots, coat and jerkin, 'what think you Dick?'

'Yes — he certainly is frightened of something it seems.'

'Maybe we will find out when he comes to see us — if he comes.'

Hardly had Will spoken than there came a light timid knock upon the door. 'Enter,' called Will

Alfred Lackton stepped quickly into the room, carrying a candle, and furtively closed the door behind him. 'I fergot, he said, ' 'ere's yer light.'

Dick Palmer took it from him and set it in an iron sconce on the wall. He turned and stared curiously at the landlord, who stood in a hesitating manner by the door. 'Come now,' said Palmer, 'what have you to tell us?'

The landlord gulped and fiddled with the rolled-up end of his shirtsleeve. Will and Dick waited patiently.

At last Lackton took a deep breath and said: 'I believe you seek this place that Tom Broughton mentioned — that the blacksmith told of in his dying breath?'

'Yes — you know we do,' snapped Will.

'Toby-Joy — what and where is it?'

'Ah-h,' whined the landlord, 'that I don't know, but maybe I can 'elp you — p'raps I can assist you.'

'Well — and what do you know?'

The landlord peered around the room, put his ear to the door and listened for a moment, then turned back and said breathlessly: 'The Monastery Inn, near Slinford in Sussex — ask there,' and with these words he opened the door and was gone.

'Can you remember that name, Dick?' asked Will quickly,

'Yes, I'll remember it — the Monastery Inn, Slinford, Sussex. Do you know where Slinford is?'

'I think so — it's almost due south of here.'

'Good,' grunted Palmer, and divesting himself of his top garments he threw himself down upon his bed beneath the little window.

Will Snell yawned and composed himself for slumber. 'I wonder what we shall find there?' he mused, half to himself.

'Yes, it will be interesting,' murmured Dick, quenching the candle, 'but what I think is most strange is why have our names been broadcasted on the high road?'

'Yes — that's a poser.' grunted Will in a faint voice and immediately there followed a gentle snore. The great man was asleep.

Palmer's thoughts flew swiftly back to the outskirts of London and Jeanette, his wife, and he wondered how she was faring — alone with Nicholas Wilken in the house. Dick knew he could rely on the boy to protect his wife — even to sacrifice his life if need be, for Nicholas worshipped his mistress. This was the first time, however, that Palmer had been away from his home for any length of time and he was uneasy and would be glad when he could return.

He soon dropped off to sleep and in a little while he dreamed of faint scufflings about the inn, of a cry and of a clatter of hooves in the yard. Then there was a silence and he slept peacefully, but soon he dreamed of the clip-clop of horses' hooves again on the cobbles of the yard. They grew louder, the momentum increased and then they gradually faded away into nothingness and Dick Palmer fell into a deep slumber, which was oblivious to such fanciful dreams.

3

The grey light of dawn lay about the inn when Dick Palmer awoke the next morning. Heavy breathing in the bed next to him indicated that Will Snell was still asleep. Dick glanced across at his friend and noticed with amusement that Will's large feet protruded some distance out of the end of his bed.

The grey light slowly changed to a translucent orange glow as the sun rose, and in a little while the birds in the nearby trees began their joyful early morning chorus. Dick listened to the peaceful sound awhile and then he was struck by the strange silence that lay upon the inn. Surely the landlord and his daughter should be up and doing at this hour? He sat up and listened intently, but except for Will's sonorous breathing and the twitter and singing of the birds outside there was complete quietness.

The whole inn appeared still and dead,

not a sound reached Palmer's ears and, with a frown he jumped out of bed, washed and shaved in the water in an earthenware jar and dressed. As he fastened his waistcoat he stared down into the stable yard, searching for some sign of life, but there was none. Then he noticed that the stable door was wide open and knowing that no conscientious ostler would ever think of leaving the door open during the night, Dick Palmer realised that something was seriously wrong in the Grasshopper Inn.

He stepped quickly across to Will and gave him a rough shake. A loud snort, grunt and gasp and the giant was sitting up staring bleary-eyed around the room. The sun now had fully risen and a shaft of light lay like a string of glittering jewels across his bed, and he blinked and shaded his eyes, then gave a mighty yawn.

'Wake up, Will,' Dick snapped, 'there is something amiss in the inn — there's no life.'

'Eh?' grunted Will.

'The inn — it seems dead.'

'What hour is it?' asked the giant,

gathering up his great bulk from the bed.

'Nigh on seven, I reckon.'

'Huh — the landlord should be up by now. A moment my friend and I'm with you.'

Pulling on his riding boots and struggling into his jerkin and coat Will was ready, and together they went to the door. Will opened it quietly and they both listened for some sound to indicate people were moving about the inn on their morning tasks, but the stillness and complete lack of noise of any kind was most apparent and now seemed to take on an evil, foreboding aspect.

Will stepped out into the passage, followed by Palmer and crept towards the stairs with a stealth surprising for one of his size. He reached the top of the stairs and descended them, step by step, with Dick Palmer close behind. Fingering his great sailor's knife in his belt as he went, Will had almost reached the bottom when he stopped abruptly and sucked in his breath in a low whistle. And Dick, glancing out into the silent taproom, gasped with horror.

Hanging by a rope attached to one of the great beams was the landlord, Alfred Lackton. His feet just touched the timbered floor and his face was distorted in a ghastly fashion.

Leaping across the room and whipping out his knife at the same time, Will slashed through the rope with one great sweep of his arm and Alfred Lackton crumpled to the floor like an empty sack.

The two men stared down in silence for a moment or two at the lifeless body and then Palmer noticed a tiny piece of paper pinned to the dead man' shirt. He stooped and tore it away, and with Will looking over his shoulder, read the scrawled message that was written thereon. It went thus:

He who telleth of Toby-Joy,
Shall die by rope, knife or spiked boy.

Dick exchanged glances with Will and without a word pocketed the note for later detailed inspection. They glanced warily around the taproom, wondering whether the killer still lurked in the shadows that lay between the sizzling bands of sunlight that streamed in through the windows. The stillness and silence was oppressive and the general air of the place seemed to indicate that the inn was as empty of life as a tomb.

'Now I remember a dream I had last night,' said Dick suddenly.

'A dream?' queried Will.

'Yes — it was of scufflings and the clatter of horses in yonder yard.'

'Aha — it was this you heard,' murmured Will, waving at the body of the landlord, 'whilst you were asleep.'

'Yes, it looks like it.'

'Come, let us search the inn,' said Will in a grim voice. 'You take a peep in the bedrooms and I'll search the kitchens and the stable.'

Palmer nodded, but before he moved off he remarked: 'What has happened to Mary, I wonder?'

Will Snell shrugged his great shoulders. 'I dare not hazard a guess — something evil I fear.'

'And what about this fellow Nodding Ned?'

'Yes — you rightly ask what about him,' grunted Will, and he strode off towards the rear of the inn, the knife back in his belt and now a pistol clutched in his fist. Dick Palmer drew his own weapon and climbed the stairs. There were only four bedrooms in the little inn and in a few moments Dick had entered each one without discovering a single sign of life. He returned to the bar again and walked out to the back looking for Will.

The great man was sat at the table in the kitchen a large hunk of meat clasped in his hands and, as Palmer entered, his jaws were in the act of tearing away a piece. He looked up and grinned. 'Sit down, Dick, we must have a bite to eat afore we take the road again.'

'Really, Will — can you eat whilst out there lies a strangled body?'

'Nay, Dick, a man has to appease his appetite dead man or no. Here, have a piece,' and Will tore off a bone and handed it to his friend.

'I must admit I am hungry,' murmured Palmer, accepting the bone. There was silence as the two men crunched and gnawed away at their breakfast. At last Will had finished and he followed it down with a glass of water. 'Did you find evidence of anybody having slept in the bedrooms?' he asked Palmer.

'Not a whisker. Nodding Ned was not as sleepy as he appeared.

'No doubt he's the killer.'

'Yes — one of the Toby-Joy coves. Did you look in the stable?'

'Yes. Our steeds are safe and well quartered.'

Dick Palmer cleaned off the remainder of the meat from the bone. 'Come, then, let us be away. I reckon it's not safe to abide hereabouts, else we shall be taken for the killer.'

They let themselves out through the kitchen door, crossed the yard and entered the little stable at the rear. The two horses, upon seeing their masters, pranced around in great delight and Red Ruby gave a shrill whinny of pleasure.

'Ha,' quoth Will, 'they seem mighty pleased to see us — unusually so. I reckon they have been frightened in the night.'

They saddled their horses immediately,

led them out into the yard and mounted. In a moment they had dug in their spurs and were trotting out on to the high road.

As they turned the corner into the high street of Nobham they came upon any number of villagers dashing hither and thither, and generally about the place there was a great air of activity.

Will swore. 'It's market day,' he growled, 'and I think dangerous for us to ride through the village at this hour — we would call attention.'

They halted and stared in consternation at the throng of noisy villagers. 'Quick,' whispered Palmer suddenly seeing a narrow track by the side of a nearby cottage, 'let us cut down yonder lane.' And he spurred ahead, leading the way, and in a short while they were trotting down a narrow track bordered by high hedgerows. The two men soon found that the track led out to the village fields.

Will Snell glanced up at the sun and remarked: 'We're travelling south, Dick — it's the way we need to go for Sussex and Slinfold.'

They rode on past large, open fields

and a number of small, enclosed fields, for the latter system at this time was spreading throughout the country. The landscape was undulating and pleasant to look upon and the whole scene was one of peaceful prosperity.

At last they came out on to a proper highway and here they were able to increase their pace to an easy gallop. Within a little while the fields began to give way to more wooded country as the two men drew further away from the village of Nobham. The sun rose higher and the morning passed by and Will and Dick suddenly realised they were hungry again.

'Look out for an inn, Dick.'

'Right,' replied Palmer, 'I'm mighty thirsty and hungry again.'

It was some time later that they came upon a tiny tavern at the side of the high road and almost hidden by a great oak tree. Dismounting, they tied their steeds to a post at the front and entered the dark, rather gloomy and musty smelling taproom. It was so dark in this place that Will and Dick, after the bright sunshine outside, momentarily could see very little, and so they can be excused for not noticing a small man leap up from his seat near the bar and silently disappear out the back.

When their eyes at last had become used to the sombre dimness within the tavern they espied a large, black haired man with enormous gold earrings standing motionless behind the bar, eyeing them in a most unfriendly manner. They stared at each other for several moments, rather as one does when sizing up an adversary before battle, and then Will cried: 'Ha, landlord, we require a meal. Do you provide such?'

The fellow hesitated, glanced about him, then nodded and retired through a low doorway at the side of the bar. Dick Palmer sat down at a table, but Will remained standing. 'Nay, Dick,' the giant grunted, 'let us seat ourselves outside in the sun. I don't like the smell of this tavern — it would put me off my food.'

Dick Palmer smiled up at his friend, for Will's fastidiousness in these matters came often as a surprise to the younger man, for he did not associate the large-limbed Will Snell with dainty fancies. 'As you wish,' Dick replied.

They opened the tavern door and returned to the bright sunshine outside, and the change from the musty, dark taproom to the fresh, green countryside that they now beheld was most refreshing.

Will had already seated himself on a rickety chair by a rickety table and was waiting impatiently for the refreshments to arrive. As Dick Palmer seated himself opposite, Will leaned across and whispered: 'I dislike this place — there is something queer about it. I am going to try and surprise our friend 'Golden Earrings' — keep your peepers on him and see if he acts at all strangely.'

Palmer nodded and in a minute the big, black-bearded fellow appeared carrying two plates of cold chicken, potatoes and greens. He placed these down unceremoniously on the table and made as if to leave. Dick licked his dry lips, stared at the table, and cried: 'Nay, man — what about some ale?'

Golden Earrings stopped and glared

back. 'You ordered no ale,' he growled.

Dick Palmer returned his malevolent stare. 'That's true,' he cried, 'but surely you don't think we should eat without drink?'

Golden Earrings muttered beneath his breath and stamped back into the tavern.

'He's a mighty strange landlord,' commented Dick.

'It's a mighty strange place altogether,' said Will.

They gazed across the road, which was no more than a track with its great pot-holes everywhere, at the copse upon the other side, wherein a multitudinous number of birds flitted from bough to bough in the slanting rays of the sun, now and again breaking forth into a shrill chatter of song.

Golden Earrings reappeared carrying the necessary tankards of ale. He set them down with apparent great haste and made as if to retire. Dick Palmer lifted his tankard and drank greedily.

'Tell me,' said Will Snell, arresting the retreat of the landlord, 'do you know hereabouts well?'

Golden Earrings stopped and half-turned, staring at Will suspiciously, but the giant had a most affable look upon his face. 'I do,' he replied.

'Maybe you can help me then,' continued Will pleasantly, leaning back in his chair so that it creaked in a truly ominous wav, and Palmer feared it was going to suddenly collapse. 'Have you heard of a place that goes by the name of Toby-Joy?'

Quite abruptly the face of the landlord went blank and he replied at once in a stony voice: 'No — I've never 'eard of it.' And with that he continued on his way and disappeared into the tavern.

Will Snell looked at his young friend questioningly. 'Huh,' grunted Dick, 'surely when you are asked a question you furrow your brow and give some thought to the matter. Not he — as blank as a board and swift with his answer. He might just as well have said he *had* heard of Toby-Joy!'

'As I thought,' replied Will, quaffing his ale with great speed. 'Come on, finish your meal and let's be on our way — I don't like this neighbourhood.'

They emptied their plates and their tankards and then Dick called out for the landlord. Golden Earrings appeared again, still glaring aggressively. Palmer enquired how much they owed him and, upon being told, he threw the money down on the table and strode straight past the landlord towards his steed. Will followed without a glance at mine host and in a short while the two men had mounted their horses and were cantering down the lane. Glancing back Dick saw the landlord still at the door staring after them.

'A proper rum cove,' growled Will.

'Yes,' replied Palmer thoughtfully, 'and I think we had best take care the rest of the journey.'

Will Snell looked quickly at his young friend, as they entered open country again, and then remarked: 'I see what you mean, Dick.'

Palmer suddenly delved into his coat pocket and produced the piece of paper they had found on the body of Alfred Lackton. He read this again to himself and then remarked: 'What is the meaning,

43

Will, of 'spiked boy'?'

'Read the verse again to me, Dick.'

And so Palmer read out loud the short message:

> *He who telleth of Toby-Joy,*
> *Shall die by rope, knife or spiked boy.*

'Nay,' quoth Will, 'spiked boy — I have no idea, never heard of the words.'

Dick pocketed the slip of paper again. 'No doubt we shall find the answer before many a day has passed.'

They rode on in silence, both dwelling thoughtfully on the strange rhyme, but neither realising how near one of them was to receiving a foretaste of the terrible power of the 'spiked boy.'

The lane meandered on between high hedgerows with fields and meadows stretching away on each side, and now and then the two horsemen left the bright countryside to enter dark woods, only to reappear within a few moments in the warm sunlight again. It was on one such occasion that leaving the still silence of a thick copse they found they had caught up with a horse and cart, clattering in a merry fashion along the rough lane.

A large, fat boy sat on top of a pile of hay, the reins in his chubby hands and singing away at the top of his shrill, squeaky voice. Dick and Will rode up on each side of him, and Will bellowed out: 'Ha, fatty — and what have you to be so cheerful about?'

The fat boy, with the rattle of the cart, had not heard them ride up and he nearly fell off his perch with surprise at the sudden appearance of two strangers. His big, brown, round eyes grew rounder in his plump face as he gazed fearfully from one to the other.

'I — I dun know,' he stammered.

'Come, come, fatty,' cried Will, grinning, 'we're friends — you have nothing to be frightened of.'

Somewhat reassured, the fat boy swallowed hard. 'Nay, sir. I thought you were some of these tewwibble robbers.'

'Dear, dear,' quoth Will, glancing meaningly across at Dick, 'do we look like such rogues?'

The fat boy glanced quickly at Will and

then at Palmer and said: 'Nay, nay, you be pwoper gentlemen, sir, that I can see now.'

'We're travelling to the coast on business,' Will told him. 'But you say there are robbers in these parts?'

'Oh yes, sir, oh yes — the country is infested with 'em. It's dangerous to wide abword 'ereabouts unpwotected,' and with this remark the fat boy reached behind him and pulled out a great, rusty blunderbuss and laid it gingerly at his side.

Will stared at this mighty weapon in some amazement and he pinched his red beard to hide the smile that hovered about his lips. Dick, upon the other side and partly out of sight of the fat boy, grinned broadly at the thought of the youth trying to use the baby cannon.

'Tell us more of the robbers, pal,' said Will, 'for it seems we had better be prepared.'

'The countwy is overwun with 'em — and nobody knows who they are. They wob an' then disappear.'

'Has the law nothing to say?' asked Will.

The fat boy grunted and spat in disgust at his nag's tail and swelled his chest with his new-found importance. 'Yes, there are some h'officers 'ereabouts as I know well enough meself, 'cos I saw four of 'em this morn.'

'Did you now,' said Will quickly, 'and where might this be?'

'Why it was back along the woad several miles.' And with this remark the fat boy glanced back over his shoulder from his elevated position on top of the pile of hay. 'Talk of the devil,' he cried, 'but this looks like them widing over yonder hill this vewy moment!'

Dick Palmer gave a cry of alarm and Will Snell swivelled in his saddle and stared back along the dusty lane between the tall, green hedgerows. Sure enough four riders hove into view, travelling at a fast pace towards them.

Will Snell cursed and glanced about him for some means of escape, but beyond the almost impenetrable hedgerows there stretched on either side fields of green corn and pasture land. Ahead was the winding lane; they could only go

47

forward and, whatever they did, they would draw immediate attention to themselves, Dick Palmer quickly realized their predicament and with compressed lips he reached for the pistol.

4

Suddenly Will Snell produced his pistol and, cocking it cried to the fat boy: 'Pull into the side, my fat friend, and don't speak 'til yonder riders have passed by.'

The fat boy gave a startled jump and stared down at the pistol levelled menacingly at him and, seeing the fierce look in Will's blue eyes, he quickly did as the big stranger commanded.

'But, sir,' he wailed, 'I thought you said — '

'Be quiet,' snapped Will, 'and all will go well with you, but say another word and this shot will split your head.'

The fat boy gasped and the horse and cart came to rest on the grass verge, with Dick Palmer between it and the hedge. Dick wondered what plan Will had in mind, but he said nothing and remained still and silent. Will replaced his pistol in his pocket and awaited the arrival of the four peace officers.

In a moment they drew abreast and Will called out in a cheerful manner: 'Ha' I given you enough room, gennelmen?'

The leading officer, a black haired fellow with a squint, pulled up and glared at him. 'Yes, you have, which is most polite, and who are you?'

'Me?' cried Will, 'why Farmer Scradge at your service, sir — I am just taking some hay to my cow-shed.'

The officer looked at him suspiciously, then at Dick Palmer. 'And who is he?'

'David?' roared Will in, it seemed, an unnecessarily loud voice, 'why, he is my dear and beloved son!'

The officer next squinted at the fat boy, who appeared most frightened, his great round eyes full of terror. The officer, however, mistook this for fear of himself and as a consequence was somewhat pleased. Abruptly he dug in his spurs, waved forward his three men, and then galloped off again down the lane and in a short while he disappeared in a cloud of dust.

Dick Palmer gave a long, audible sigh of relief and he rode forward and joined

Will upon the other side of the cart. 'Well, well, Mr. Scradge,' he exclaimed, grinning, 'that was handled very nicely indeed.'

Will gave a broad smile and fingered his red beard, feeling highly satisfied himself with the way he had handled the incident. 'Yes, Dick, it was a simple ruse but it worked.'

Palmer nodded. 'Now, I think, we had better be on our way, else this lad will be broadcasting the affair to all and sundry before we are out of the neighbourhood.'

'Quite true, Dick,' Will replied. 'Hey, fatty,' he called to the youth, 'are we right for Slinfold in Sussex?'

The fat boy blinked and said in a surly tone: 'Yes, wogue, it's straight forward and you come to the main woad which bwings you there.'

'Many, many thanks — and cheer up — may there be vast repast awaiting when you get home.'

The fat boy grunted and stared at them with a hurt expression in his round eyes. Will waved cheerily to him and then he and Dick Palmer were galloping off along the lane, not very far behind the four peace officers.

The two men had ridden but three furlongs when the landscape suddenly darkened and a cool breeze sprang up, which was most refreshing on their tanned faces. Dick glanced up at the sun and saw that it was obscured by a long, black cloud with ominous trailing edges.

'It looks as if we're in for a heavy shower,' he said.

The red-headed giant nodded and then pointed forward at a large wood they were approaching. 'Yes, Dick but we should reach yonder wood before the rain is upon us.'

Palmer glanced across the fields to the distant hills in the west and over their summits could be seen what appeared like a wispy curtain of trailing strings, for the cloud was over that point and it was already raining there. He realised that within a minute the rain would be upon them.

'Come on, Will, loosen your sails else we shall be soaked.'

They dug in their spurs and rode neck

and neck at a swift gallop along the lane and as they reached the forest the rains swept down with an almighty hiss and immediately the lane was turned into a muddy track. The thick foliage of the trees provided excellent cover and the travellers could hear the raindrops splashing on the leaves above. In the forest it seemed as if it were nearly dusk, though it was yet late afternoon. The two men slowed to a trot, taking it easily and hoping that by the time they reached the opposite side of the forest the cloudburst would have passed over.

They had ridden nearly half way through when with startling suddenness four masked horsemen appeared silently out of the undergrowth and, before either could as much as reach for a weapon, they were beset upon with great fierceness. Dick Palmer tried to spur forward and ride down his two attackers, but clutching fingers dragged him from his horse. As he fell he glanced quickly at Will to see how he was faring, and with a shock he observed the giant, too, being dragged from his steed. Palmer saw at the same time that one of Will's attackers was as big as Will himself.

Dick fought with all his lithe strength, wriggling out of each grasp with which the two men tried to hold him, and then he had the satisfaction to hear one of the men give an anguished cry as his head jolted back from a vicious thrust from Dick's fist. He almost managed to scramble to his feet, but out of the corner of his eye he saw the other ruffian let loose a blow at his head with a heavy club, and he dived to one side to escape it.

Abruptly a strange, high-pitched voice rang out. 'Curses on the Lady, this cove shall feel the boy!' A scream of pain rang out, echoing down the lane in a chilling, shivering manner and Dick Palmer's blood ran cold, for he realised the scream came from Will Snell.

Dick now fought with maniacal ferocity, lashing out with his fists with all the power of his sinewy frame and momentarily his two assailants were thrown from him. As Palmer leaped to his feet and was about to draw his pistol, a shot rang out and a sudden silence followed. Then there was a scurry of feet and, as Palmer cocked his pistol, the four robbers swiftly leaped on their steeds and in a moment were galloping away down the lane.

Dick fired after them, but in the poor light his shot went wide; he drew his second pistol and then realised the futility of a second bullet, for the four men were now well out of range.

Palmer turned and an awful chill ran down his spine when he saw Will Snell lying motionless on the ground, deep lacerations down the side of his face and blood spattered everywhere.

He sprang forward to his friend's side, anxiously wondering what to do, for Will was unconscious. It was then that Dick heard the sound of horses approaching from the opposite direction and looking up quickly saw three riders moving towards him, one with a smoking pistol in his hand. Palmer realised then from whence the shot had come and he awaited their arrival, still on the alert for any indication of hostility.

One of the newcomers was old and frail

looking and wore a black wig, the other man was young and long of limb and it was he who had fired the shot: the third was a woman. They dismounted silently and the woman ran forward and knelt down beside Dick Palmer and surveyed his friend's wounds with consternation.

'Oh,' cried she, 'he is wounded most terribly,' and as she spoke Will opened his eyes and stared blankly up at her. She turned to Palmer and he noticed then that she had long golden-red tresses, much the same colour as Will's comely but strong features and sparkling green eyes.

'We must place him on his steed,' she exclaimed, taking charge. 'Jeremy,' she called to the young man, 'help me, will you.' The tall fellow strolled over, and he and Palmer, with some effort, lifted Will as gently as they could on to his black stallion.

Palmer now felt more inclined to trust the three strangers and he said briefly: 'Where to?'

'To our home,' the girl replied and they all mounted their steeds, and the girl rode up alongside Will and supported him. They started forward slowly and traversed the wood in silence. The rain had stopped and everything became brighter and here and there white shafts of light broke through the foliage into the lane.

In a short while they left the forest and came out into the fresh, green country-side and with the change Dick Palmer's spirits rose and he threw off the cloak of anxious depression that had enveloped him upon seeing his great friend sorely wounded.

The old man spoke: 'Young fellow — did the rogues take much?'

Dick looked at the old man, noting how frail he appeared and his large black wig seemed incongruous on his small wizened head.

'No, they took nothing,' he replied. He glanced then across at Will and saw that his big friend was slumped in the saddle, silent and obviously in pain. The girl rode at his side, her eyes upon him continu-ously watching for any indication that he might fall. Palmer felt grateful to her. Next he inspected the young man riding at his side. His features were long and drooping and his loose fair hair added to his general lanky and rather doleful appearance.

The fellow caught Dick looking at him and he gave a slight smile and Palmer smiled quickly in return and then faced the front, deciding that he liked the three newcomers.

'I am Squire Mathering of Ewhurst,' announced the old man suddenly with some pomp. 'These,' he added, waving his thin hand at the girl and the man, 'are my children — Crimson and Jeremy.'

Palmer politely inclined his head and replied, after a little hesitation: 'Dick Palmer is my name and my wounded friend is Will Snell.' Introductions being over everybody relaxed a little and the party continued on their way along the lane.

'Do you know who these villains were?' asked Jeremy Mathering in his slow, drawling voice.

'No, I don't,' Dick replied.

The red-headed girl, Crimson Mathering, was now holding Will Snell's arm to stop him from falling off his horse and the big man's face was white beneath his tanned, weather-beaten skin. The girl had wrapped a piece of cloth, which she had produced from somewhere, twice around his head so that the gashes were hidden, but a large red patch showed that the wounds still bled profusely.

'How much farther?' asked Palmer.

'Ewhurst is around yonder corner,' quoth the Squire, 'and Mathering Manor is at the far end.'

'You can stop the night there,' said the Squire's daughter. 'This gentleman is in no condition for further travelling.'

'Thank you,' replied Palmer, thinking how amused Will would be if he could have heard himself referred to as a 'gentleman'. He glanced across at his friend wondering whether he had heard the words, but Will's head was slumped forward on his chest, his eyes staring blankly down and he seemed half unconscious.

They turned a corner and the lane immediately widened out as it passed between two irregular lines of neat red-bricked thatched cottages. This was Ewhurst, as the Squire forthwith announced. 'Mind you,' he added, looking straight at Dick with his pale, watery eyes, 'in my younger days I controlled more land here than I do now.'

'Oh,' said Palmer, not knowing what else to say.

'Yes,' said the Squire, nodding his black locks and staring at his horse's head, 'I was a man of some substance in the old days. Ha! the good old days!'

'Well, here we are,' cried Crimson Mathering cheerfully, pointing at a great iron gate set between two snug cottages. Beyond was a drive that disappeared amidst trees. Jeremy dismounted and opened the gate himself, for there appeared to be no keeper, and they rode through and along the drive. The Squire's son quickly caught up the others and in a moment the drive left the trees and ended before a long, rambling red-bricked house with high, thin chimneys and tiny windows half hidden by the low hanging eaves and odd bits of brickwork that jutted out here and there. A neat lawn was laid before the house edged with flowering borders.

A big bald fellow with one eye came to the door as they dismounted and raised his black bushy eyebrows upon seeing the two newcomers.

'Bob,' said the Squire imperiously, 'take our steeds to the stables and then prepare two of the guest rooms.'

Bob stared in surprise with his one blue eye and glanced at the lady and she nodded silently, as if confirming the Squire's order. Bob lumbered forward, assisted Jeremy and Dick to lower Will to the ground and then ambled round the back of the house with the five horses.

Crimson Mathering led the way into the manor and Palmer and the Squire's son carried Will Snell into a cosy little room with low timber beams and a big hearth with stone seats each side. On the white walls were any number of hunting pictures and the tiny window in an alcove looked out upon the lawn in front of the house. There was a quiet, peaceful air about the room. Will was placed in a great chair near the hearth and still he seemed little conscious of what was taking place around him.

'We'll put him to bed directly Bob has prepared the room,' exclaimed the Squire's daughter.

'It's very kind of you, Madam, and I can assure you it is much appreciated,' replied Dick sincerely. 'Such hospitality is rare indeed these days.'

'A pleasure, young fellow,' said the Squire, seating himself in a chair by the window. 'My abode is always open to the weary traveller.'

Dick bowed slightly and at that moment Bob appeared in the doorway to announce in a loud voice that the guest rooms were now ready for the 'gennelmen'. Will was half carried up the narrow winding staircase to his bedroom and there Dick Palmer was left alone with him. Crimson Mathering, however, turned on the threshold and said:

'When he's in bed then I'll come and attend to his wounds. You, good sir,' she added, 'will sup with us downstairs within the hour.'

'Thank you, good lady,' replied Dick,

'you are most considerate.'

When she had closed the door Dick Palmer glanced out of the window, for he had not realised it was so late and he saw that the sun had long since set. He turned to Will Snell and found that worthy trying to take off his riding boots.

'Ha, Will, so you are conscious at last.'

The giant looked up and grinned wryly: 'Nay, Dick, but I have been conscious all along.'

'Well, well, have you now, and how d'you feel?'

'Fair to middling, Dick — fair to middling, but I admit I shall be glad to climb into this 'ere bed.'

Palmer assisted his friend to undress and a few moments later Will Snell gave a great sigh as he lay back on the pillow. 'Off you go, Dick, and tell her I'm ready!'

'Ready for what? I reckon you're a lucky man have such a lady to tend to your injury.'

Will gave a broad grin. 'Yes, Dick, so do I.' Then Will's smile faded and he said quietly: 'When you come to bed yourself, Dick, visit me here and we will have a few words about our recent adventure. I have drawn one or two conclusions and I am of the inclination that this mystery which we propose solving is a mighty wicked and evil thing.'

Palmer had never heard Will Snell speak before in such a serious and solemn manner, and with the giant's sobering words ringing in his ears he left to call Crimson Mathering, having promised Will he would return after supper.

Several hours later, when the moon was at its zenith, Dick Palmer wearily climbed the narrow staircase to bed, having supped most excellently and drank some exceedingly fine wine. At the table Crimson Mathering had done most of the talking, flashing her green eyes and shaking her golden tresses at each and all of them at the same time. Twice during the meal she suddenly sat up and ran up the stairs to see how her patient was, her conscientiousness in this respect surprising Palmer.

Upon entering his friend's bedroom Dick found Will staring out of the window in a strange, distant manner. The giant started when he saw Palmer standing at the foot of his bed and seemed a little embarrassed.

'Oh, Dick, I did not hear you enter. I was far away thinking on strange things.'

'That's a fine bandage you have wrapped round your head, Will — you look like a mummy!'

'Yes, she makes a good nurse.'

Palmer sat down on the edge of the bed and stared thoughtfully at Will Snell, noting the humorous picture the latter presented, with his red beard protruding from his bandage so that he looked like an overgrown baby. Dick remarked: 'The Matherings don't seem to have heard of us.'

'So it appeared when you told them on the high road this afternoon,' nodded Will. 'We are quite safe here I have no doubt. I have told Miss Mathering the reason we are in this neighbourhood.'

'Ah, you have, and what did she say?'

'Very little. She has heard of this gang and even 'Toby-Joy', but, like everybody else, it seems, knows nothing more.'

'What about the Squire and his son?'

'She said she would tell them and seemed confident they would understand our position.'

'But don't they know anything else?'

'She is not certain but says the matter can be discussed tomorrow.'

Will Snell suddenly sat up in bed and leaned toward his friend, and now he spoke in a low voice: 'Dick, did you notice these wounds when I was in the wood?'

'That I did — lacerations, as if you had been clawed by an animal or something.'

Will nodded, his blue eyes gleaming. 'C'rect, my friend; and you remember Tom Broughton, the blacksmith of Nobham?'

'I do,' replied Palmer.

'An' do you remember my description of his wounds?'

'Yes — hah, I see what you mean. They were like yours.'

'Now, Dick, may I ask you to produce that little verse we found on the poor landlord's body at the Grasshopper?'

Dick felt in one of his waistcoat pockets and in a moment found the piece of paper to which Will Snell referred.

'Read it to me again, Dick.'

Palmer did as he was requested.

He who telleth of Toby-Joy,

Shall die by rope, knife or spiked boy.

'Ha, that's it, Dick; that's it, I tell you — spiked boy!'

Dick Palmer stared at Will's intent expression. 'You mean it was the spiked boy that wounded you and the blacksmith?'

'C'rect, Dick.'

'But what is it — what is the spiked boy?'

'Ah, I don't know that, but I saw faintly the rogue that dealt the blow and he was a mighty big cove.'

'Yes, I saw him too, and I saw him swing his arm and then you let out a scream.'

'It was unpleasantly painful I might tell you, Dick,' said Will Snell, leaning back against his pillow again and staring out of the window, a strange look in his eyes. At last he turned to the fair-headed man again sitting on the side of his bed and he exclaimed very deliberately:

'I reckon I'll be marked for life, Dick,

and like all of us, being fond of my visage, ugly thing though it may be, my feelings towards this cove are not exactly friendly.' Will said the last words in a low, matter of fact voice, staring intently at Dick Palmer. Now, with a deadly glitter in his eyes, he added slowly: 'It's because of this, Dick, that I intend to seek out this vile rogue and — kill him!'

5

The following evening Dick Palmer strolled in the pretty grounds of Mathering Manor with Jeremy whilst upstairs in the house Will Snell continued his day long battle with the Squire's daughter on whether he should rise from bed or not. Will contended that he was fit enough to get up and Miss Mathering contended most emphatically that he was not. So far the girl had succeeded in keeping him in bed but every time she went up to see him, which was quite often, the argument was renewed with vehement energy.

Their voices could be heard now as Dick walked between the tall trees at the end of the lawn. Palmer grinned up at the lanky young man at his side: 'Your sister is the first person, I think, Will has met who refuses to give in to him.'

'Yes,' nodded Jeremy. 'Crimson is quite a wild and stubborn girl.'

'Same with Will.'

'She will let him get up tomorrow no doubt, but I think she's wise to keep him there today, for his wounds were no flea-bite.'

'He is mighty keen to track down this rascal with the spiked boy.'

'Most understandable,' said Jeremy in his leisurely voice, 'an' I don't fancy to be in the fellow's shoes.'

The two men stopped and turned as they heard footsteps coming through the copse from the direction of the manor. A large, round, bald head appeared over a bush followed in a moment by a single bright eye, as Bob, the Mathering's servant cum valet cum ostler, joined them, a secretive look upon his battered countenance, for Bob Flint had once been a pugilist of some renown.

' 'Scuse me, Master Jeremy — Master Dick,' he said in his gruff voice, 'but what I 'ave to tell you, Master Dick, I think will interest you.'

'Oh, and what's that, Bob?' asked Palmer.

'Well, I 'eard from Mistress Crimson what you seek and that you intend visitin' the Monastery Inn at Slinfold in Sussex.'

'That's correct.'

'Well,' said Bob, moving closer and eyeing them confidentially with his one eye, 'when I 'ears what your name is, Master Dick, and that o' your wounded friend it put me in mind of what, I think you'll agree, was an interesting affair that I sees at the Monastery Inn not long since.'

The one-eyed servant had swiftly obtained the attention of the two men.

'Well,' continued Bob, 'it was like this. I was sitting in the Monastery Inn with me ale minding me own business — as I allus do — when in comes three strangers. Now I might tell you,' said Bob, 'although I 'ave but this one eye — God bless it — I sees an awful lot with it, for it has got mighty dexterous, as you might say, in its job of seeing what goes on around me.

'Well, as I say, in comes these three strangers, and as I 'appen to be squatted down right near the bar I 'ears them ask the bartender in a whisper if the 'Lady' is in.'

Bob's eye was quick to see Dick Palmer

start, but the latter made no comment and so the ex-pugilist continued. 'Out comes a woman who's plump and mighty powdered and painted. Says she to one of the men: 'Ha, Glaxby, you have returned.' This fellow then says — mind, all in a whisper — 'e says with a grin: 'That's not my name me Lady, if you recollect, it's Will Snell.'

'This woman then clicks 'er teeth like as if she is annoyed. 'Of course, of course,' she mutters. 'Now come within and give me your news.'

'Thereupon they all steps out the back an' I sees 'em no more.'

Bob Flint looked at Dick Palmer questioningly. 'That's my story, Master Dick — of any use to you?'

'It certainly is, Bob,' cried Palmer, 'thank you many times — the Monastery Inn seems to be the headquarters of this gang.'

'Yes, that is just what I reckoned meself.'

'Tell me, Bob,' exclaimed Palmer, 'what was the woman like?'

'Nay, I cannot tell you more,' grunted

Bob; 'the lanterns were weak and all I could see was she was plump and proper done up — petticoats and powder.'

'Thank you again, Bob — you have been most helpful.'

'It's a pleasure, Master Dick,' replied the one-eyed servant amiably, and he stamped off back to the house.

'What do you think it all means, Dick?' asked Jeremy as they returned to the manor.

'I don't know, but this I do know: I shall sip ale at the Monastery Inn tonight.'

'Alone, Dick? But that's madness. Let me accompany you.'

Dick Palmer glanced sideways at the tall frame of Jeremy Mathering, who was perhaps a year younger than Palmer himself. He wondered what the long limbed youth would be like in a tight corner, in a fight, and he decided Jeremy lacked no pluck and, after all, two pistols would be better than one.

'It's a good idea, Jeremy; it would be, as you say, dangerous to enter such a place alone. Let's set out after supper then.'

Jeremy Mathering gave one of his rare slow smiles they entered the manor. At that moment Crimson Mathering descended the stairs.

'Nay, Dick, that friend of yours, Will Snell, be the most stubborn and most awkward cuss I have ever met.' With this remark she hastened past them and out to the back of the house, shaking her golden locks, and in a moment could be heard telling the cook what to prepare for 'Willy' upstairs.

'Have you a good steed, Jeremy?'

'Yes an excellent grey mare, though to be sure not as good as that chestnut mare of yours. Where did she come from?'

'Believe it or not,' replied Palmer, grinning, 'a highwayman in Newgate Prison gave her to me before he did the Tyburn Hornpipe.'

'You mean — before he was hanged at Tyburn?'

'Yes, it was a parting gift, and I have never had a better one.'

Later Dick climbed the staircase to visit Will Snell. The giant was sitting up in bed reading a newspaper. 'Hello,

Dick, how are you?'

'Fine, Will, but how are you?'

'Excellent, friend. This woman is a pest; she refuses to let me get up.'

'Too bad,' commiserated Dick; then he added: 'I have some news, Will,' and he repeated Bob Flint's story.

'Ah! Now that's interesting.'

'This is my opinion, Will. This woman, for what reason we have yet to discover, sent these four rogues to collect us; they were not trying to kill but to kidnap us.'

Will stared a short while at his young friend. 'It's possible, Dick, but what about this blow?' and Will indicated his bandaged head.

'That was in anger, Will, at finding it no easy job to take you. Mind what that big villain said: 'Curses on the Lady, this cove shall feel the boy'.'

'You always were the bright one, Dick; you seem to have something there. But who's this woman, then? Why does she seek us?'

'I don't know. However, Jeremy and I intend visiting the Monastery Inn this night to sample their ale.'

Will Snell jerked forward in his bed and suddenly a painful expression entered his eyes and with a groan partly pain and partly frustration, he fell back against the pillow again. 'Curse it, you have all the luck, Dick,' he grunted enviously.

Following supper Bob Flint went out to saddle Dick and Jeremy's horses and in a little while he brought them around to the front of the house. The two men took care to arm themselves with three pistols apiece and a knife each and, having made sure their pistols were properly charged, they mounted their steeds.

'Best o' luck, masters!' cried Bob and he thereupon released the bridles. Immediately the two men, at a touch of their spurs, galloped down the drive, turning before they passed out of sight to wave to the Squire and his daughter standing in the little porch of the manor.

Jeremy headed out of the gate and turned due south away from the village and soon they were traversing a rolling heath-like country sparsely covered with woodlands. Red Ruby was in a jubilant mood and Palmer had to restrain her, else she would have leaped ahead of Jeremy's grey mare.

It was a peaceful summer evening and as they rode they could hear the birds singing joyfully in the trees on either side of the highway. The journey was a pleasant one and the two men said little, enjoying to the full the cool breeze on their faces as they galloped along.

Dick Palmer took to thinking of his wife at their home near London and he wondered what she was doing at the present time — perhaps tending the garden with the help of Nicholas Wilken, and Palmer realised that Jeanette was perfectly safe when the boy was present. 'Naughty Nick' was a brave lad and should anybody molest them they would find the youth a handful indeed!

His thoughts were interrupted by Jeremy: 'Look yonder, Dick, and you'll see the ruined monastery from which the inn takes its name.'

They had reached the brow of a hill and over to the east on the top of a knoll there stood the ancient ruins of a once large monastery. Below them and some distance ahead Dick could see the village of Slinfold, as Jeremy indicated, and short of the village was their objective, but it was at present obscured by trees.

The two men descended the slope at a canter, now very watchful, and abruptly they came upon the Monastery Inn. It was a plain, grey-stoned place with four tiny windows but with a surprisingly large and strong door fitted with massive iron studs. This, Dick realised, was supposed to represent a monastery door. Behind the inn were stables and outhouses bordered by tall, thin trees. Through these trees could just be seen the ruined walls of the monastery on the solitary hill.

The door stood wide open and sounds of life came from it. The two men dismounted and tied their horses to an iron rail. Jeremy exchanged glances with Dick and together they entered the Monastery Inn. The interior was comparatively dark but that did not stop Palmer from seeing a woman suddenly rise from her stool behind the bar and, with a rustle of petticoats, move hastily away and disappear through a door at the back.

They ordered a tankard of ale each from a short wizened man who grinned at them in what was supposed to be, Palmer presumed, a pleasant manner, but it was more of a leer. Jeremy produced his briar and tinderbox and was soon puffing away in a contented fashion, and Dick noted with approval that his lanky companion was perfectly cool. Palmer himself was somewhat nervous, as was his wont, but the former highwayman could prove a most formidable adversary once there was action.

The noise they heard upon entering the inn emanated from two old farmers who sat in a corner quaffing ale in great gulps and at the same time arguing heatedly on the advantages and disadvantages of crop rotation. In another corner nearer the bar there was an empty table except for an ancient bearded gentleman, and Dick suggested they take a seat. But Jeremy lingered at the bar and when the barman reappeared from the kitchen he called him over.

'Tell me,' said Jeremy blandly, 'who is the lady we saw when we entered?'

A cunning gleam entered the little man's eyes and he paused before replying. Then: 'Why, it was Mrs. Heckley, the proprietor of this inn.'

Jeremy nodded in an unconcerned manner and joined Dick Palmer at the table. Dick leaned close to Jeremy and whispered: 'You know, it's strange, but she seems familiar.'

'Ha, you think you know her?'

'Yes, but for the life of me I can't remember where I have seen her before.'

Suddenly the ancient fellow at their side, who had been peacefully dozing, awoke and remarked in a surprisingly educated voice: 'Good evening, my fine gentlemen, and I think you are strangers hereabouts?'

'C'rect,' Palmer replied, 'we are passing through.' He glanced curiously at the old man, who sported an exceedingly fine long white beard. Dick decided at once to ask a leading question. 'We seek, my good sir, a place by the name of Toby-Joy. Have you heard of it?'

The old gentleman considered a moment and then shook his venerable head and took a sip of red wine in a small glass on the table before him. 'No, I cannot say that such a name strikes a chord in my sadly ineffective memory. Why do you ask, young man?'

Dick Palmer was about to reply when he observed the bartender leaning their way, one ear cocked and grinning like a Cheshire cat. Instead Dick drank his ale and lightly fingered one of his pistols in his capacious coat pocket. Jeremy absent-mindedly played with a loose piece of silk embroidery on his grey coat and then as the wizened bartender still leered across at them said in his drawling voice: 'Barman.'

'Yes, sire,' said the fellow, coming quickly forward.

'Barman,' repeated Jeremy, crossing his long legs beneath the table, 'as your visage reminds me of the back of a drayhorse it would please me greatly if you took it elsewhere!'

Dick Palmer gasped, gurgled and finally burst into a roar of laughter. The bartender's eyes nearly popped out of his head, his wizened face went livid and he glared in a most ferocious manner at his two customers. He glanced this way and that as if not sure what to do at such an insult and Palmer's fingers tightened on his pistol. At last with a dreadful curse he crept away muttering to the far side of the room.

Dick felt a light tap on his arm and, turning, he found the white-bearded ancient beckoning him with a long skinny finger, though Palmer sat directly next to him. The old man was looking highly pleased with himself. 'I remember,' he cried, 'I remember,' and Dick feared his strident voice would reach the bartender.

'What — what d'you remember?' asked Jeremy quickly, leaning forward.

The old gentleman beamed. 'My memory is not as bad as I thought,' he said delightedly.

'Yes, it's excellent,' breathed Palmer. 'Now tell us what have you remembered, and please speak low.'

'Toby-Joy,' said the old gentleman, his brown eyes shining brightly, 'it's the old name they used to call the monastery on yonder hill.'

'The Monastery?' queried Dick, frowning, 'but it is in ruins.'

'Yes, yes, but I remember — my grandfather told me. When it was a thriving monastery — it's nigh on two hundred years ago now — the monks used to provide refreshments and fare for passing travellers on the highway — the High Toby — and so the monastery became known throughout the county as Toby-Joy!'

There was a gleam of triumph in Dick Palmer's eyes as he called the bartender across. 'Another glass of wine, barman, for my good friend here.' With a deep scowl the wizened fellow complied with the request and then, having been paid, he slunk away, scowling more than ever.

'Dear me, dear me,' cried the old gentleman, 'but this is indeed a kind gesture, young sir. I drink to your good health,' and he took a sip of his red wine and then sat back and beamed.

'I suppose no one lives in the monastery now?' asked Jeremy.

'Oh no, certainly not. It's a complete ruin. Mind you,' added the old gentleman, 'hereabouts there is a great fear for the place; no man goes near.'

'How's that?'

'They say it's haunted by the monks — that on a dark night evil voices and laughter float about the walls. I thought they were old wives' tales,' concluded the old gentleman, 'but — ' and he leaned closer so that his beard nearly dipped in Palmer's ale — 'if the truth be known there seems there is some substance in the story for I have heard these weird sounds myself!'

6

Deciding that it would be advisable to inspect the monastery in daylight on the morrow, Dick Palmer and Jeremy Mathering, having wished the old gentleman goodnight, returned to their horses. Already it was dusk and the grey sky was covered with a myriad of twinkling stars.

They mounted their steeds and swinging them around galloped back the way they had come. As they ascended the hill Dick Palmer suddenly felt that someone was watching him. Abruptly he turned in his saddle and looked back at the Monastery Inn and for a moment he saw the white face of a woman staring at him from one of the upper windows. In another moment the face had disappeared.

Dick Palmer rode on at the side of Jeremy and spoke no word. The incident had strangely moved him, for he knew that somewhere, sometime he had seen that face before, and with this knowledge came the realisation that the face represented in his mind all that was cruel and evil. As they rode further away from the inn so the feeling of uneasiness passed away and when they entered the drive to Mathering Manor Dick was his normal self again.

Bob Flint took their horses from them and Palmer was about to go up and see Will Snell and tell him of what they had discovered at the inn when he found his way barred by Crimson Mathering.

'Are you going to speak with Willie?'

'C'rect,' replied Dick.

Crimson Mathering shook her long red tresses. 'No,' said she quite definitely.

'No? Why not?'

'Willie is asleep.'

'Oh, is he? As you will. I can tell him tomorrow.'

'What?'

Dick realised that Crimson Mathering was not intending to be kept in the dark. Patiently he recounted to her what the old gentleman at the inn had told them about the monastery.

'What does that mean?'

'It means I shall take a close look at the monastery on the morrow. I think we are on the right track. The gang's headquarters are undoubtedly somewhere in that neighbourhood.'

'Where do you think they take these poor girls they kidnap?'

'Ha! That we have yet to discover. And now I aim to retire.' Dick wished the girl goodnight and climbed the stairs to his room.

Upon the next day Crimson Mathering, following a short argument, reluctantly allowed Will Snell to get up. Will pointed out to Dick, as they sat on a bench in the garden after breakfast, if she had her way he would still be in bed come next summer. The giant naturally looked pale, for of course his wounds were not yet healed, but the sun and the fresh air soon brought colour to his cheeks and eased his aching head.

Crimson Mathering apparently had already told Will of the old gentleman's story, and so Dick added the news of the woman he had seen in the taproom of the

Monastery Inn who had seemed familiar. However Palmer did not tell his friend of the strange premonition of evil he had experienced upon observing her face at the window for he feared that Will might only laugh at the incident.

At this moment Jeremy Mathering strolled over to their bench and sat down at their side. 'How's the head, Will?' he asked.

'Fine, Jeremy, fine, thank you. I hear you've been calling some poor barman rude names!'

Jeremy's solemn face broke into a quick smile but he crossed his long legs and said nothing. Will considered the Squire's son out of the corner of his eye and he felt inclined to agree with Dick that here was a man, for all his languid manner, of some substance and one to be relied upon.

Palmer suddenly jumped to his feet. 'Come, Jeremy, let's view the ruined monastery and maybe find the solution to Toby-Joy.'

Jeremy yawned and uncoiled his great length from the low bench. 'I'm ready.

Let's hope we meet the vile rogue who did this,' and he indicated Will's bandaged head.

Palmer nodded and they made off towards the stables with Will Snell staring after them enviously and muttering beneath his breath something about 'interfering women.'

They soon came riding along the front of the manor and Dick, seeing Will sitting so dejectedly on the bench, cried out: 'Cheer up, Will, we'll bring you back a memento from the monastery.'

The giant scowled and said nothing but acknowledged Dick's wave of the hand, and then the two men had disappeared down the drive.

At the top of the hill leading down to the Monastery Inn Dick Palmer held up his hand and they came to a halt at the side of the dusty road.

'I think it would be better to cut through the trees to the monastery, Jeremy, rather than pass the inn.'

The Squire's son nodded and immediately they turned their horses into the trees and threaded their way through the wood. They could not now see the monastery and had to guess their direction but in a little while, where the wood grew thicker, they came to a gradual slope and knew this for the base of the knoll on which the monastery stood. They walked their horses between the bushes and thickets that abounded on the hill and found that the knoll was larger than at first appeared for they climbed for some time.

At last they saw the end of the wood before them and breaking out, espied the ruined walls of the monastery in a jagged square on the summit of the hill. Digging in their spurs they galloped to the top and came to a halt beneath a great wall. The two men dismounted and led their horses through a large opening, once a massive doorway, into the roofless hall of the monastery, Observing a convenient iron ring attached to a great block of stone in one of the walls, Dick tethered Red Ruby to it and Jeremy followed his example.

Leading off from the hall were various small rooms, some roofed, others not. Dick and Jeremy visited all of these, inspecting every dark corner and every niche. At the far side of the hall was another large room leading off at right angles, also roofless and with a great bush growing up in the middle of the grassy floor. The grass was a bright green and soft and velvety and the two men could see no sign of footsteps anywhere. There were ruins of smaller buildings upon the far side and in one was a deep well that was neither railed off nor covered over.

A jagged piece of wall cast a shadow over this gaping hole and, what with the bright sunshine, Jeremy failed to see it and would have fallen in, but for a great yell from Dick Palmer and his restraining hand. The Squire's son turned deathly pale and stepped back with horror from the broken edge of the well.

'Nay, but that was a near one. Thanks, Dick.'

'Pleasure, Jeremy,' Dick replied, bowing and raising his black three-cornered hat.

'You make light of the matter,' grunted Jeremy, 'but I reckon I would look silly at the bottom of yonder well.'

'Reckon you would,' agreed Dick

solemnly. 'Very silly.' He raised his hat again and scratched his fair hair, stared about the ruined monastery and frowned. 'There's nothing here, Jeremy. The old gentleman must have been mistaken. The place is dead.'

'Yes, we are wasting our time. What now?'

'Let's ride back by the road to the inn and surprise our friend the barman. We may see something new.'

They returned to the ring in the wall, untethered their horses and Palmer led the way down the track at the side of the monastery, and in a moment they were traversing the road back to the inn. On each side of them the forest lay thick and almost impregnable and the road wound hither and thither in a leisurely fashion so that at no time were the two men able to see any great distance ahead. The birds twittered and hooted all around them with great cheerfulness and Dick began to wonder whether there was after all a ruthless gang operating in the neighbour-hood. Perhaps it was their imagination and in reality life was as peaceful as it did at present appear.

Such were Palmer's thoughts when they trotted around yet another bend and all at once Red Ruby gave a shrill whinny and shied high in the air. Cursing, Palmer got her under control and then stared grimly ahead. Lying in the middle of the road was a body of a man. Quickly the two men dismounted and ran forward, and as they reached the fellow's side a sickening gasp escaped Jeremy's lips.

It was the old gentleman they had met the previous night in the Monastery Inn and the reason for Jeremy's shudder was that the man's head was completely smashed in on one side in strange, deep furrows. His white hair was white no longer but dirty red and the blood was still wet and sticky. His one undamaged eye was wide open staring up at the foliage above, and the look in that dead eye made Dick Palmer give a sudden cold shiver.

With compressed lips he stepped closer to view the remains of the old gentleman the better. He then saw a piece of paper neatly attached to the dead man's waistcoat and, with a grunt, Dick bent down and tore it away knowing full well what words were inscribed thereon.

However he read them out loud for the benefit of Jeremy:-

He who telleth of Toby-Joy,
Shall die by rope, knife or spiked boy.

A very grim expression came to Dick Palmer's face, and he said, standing over the body of the old gentleman as if in prayer: 'It's no man that can do such an act as this, Jeremy; it's a beast, a loathsome beast.'

They stood in silence for a moment and abruptly the silence was broken by a strange voice behind them.

'Yes, my good friends, how very true that is.'

Dick Palmer swung about, drawing and cocking his pistol all in one movement, at which the stranger who had ridden up quietly behind them, raised his black eyebrows in surprised admiration.

'Excellent,' saith he; 'mighty dexterous I must admit.'

The newcomer sat his horse in a lordly manner, was dressed in a black coat and waistcoat edged with gold braid and a black tricorn hat trimmed with the same material. His dark aquiline features were accentuated by a trim, pointed beard, after the French fashion, and his piercing eyes met Palmer's complacently.

'Who are you?' asked Dick

The stranger dismounted, doffed his hat and replied in a deep bass voice: 'May I introduce myself, good sir: Jonathan Stark, at your service.'

'You agree with my sentiments?' queried Palmer, eyeing Stark suspiciously.

'I certainly do. I have been seeking the owner of the 'spiked boy' this twelve-month.'

Jeremy glanced swiftly at Dick and the latter pocketed his pistol, his eyes gleaming. 'I think, Mr. Stark, we have the same object.'

The dapper newcomer nodded: 'So it seems.'

'My name is Dick Palmer and this is

Jeremy Mathering. Do you know a place hereabouts where we might discuss this matter in peace?'

'Let me see. Yes, the Black Horse Tavern is a peaceful place and they serve fine ale.'

'Good!' Dick Palmer thereupon turned and surveyed the body of the old gentleman. 'Take his legs, Jeremy, and we'll lay him in the brush.' With grim lips the two men lifted the old gentleman, carried him across to the edge of the forest and laid him amongst the bushes. As Palmer was about to turn away he caught sight of something brown lying in the grass at the edge of the road.

'Ha! What have we here!' he cried, stooping and picking it up.

Jeremy and Jonathan Stark hurried to his side and stared down at the small article he held in his hand. It was a leather belt wallet.

'Open it,' said Stark. 'I avow it was torn from one of the rogue's belts in the struggle.'

Palmer opened the wallet and drew out a number of coins and finally a tiny piece of paper. On this was written in a scrawling hand the following message:

Meet at the Inn by the River at Midnight.

The note was signed by 'Simon Pendexter.' The three men stared at the words for several moments.

'Who is Simon Pendexter?' asked Palmer.

'Don't you know?' queried Stark in a surprised tone, and his lips suddenly tightened and a strange brilliance entered his dark eyes. 'Simon Pendexter is the man I seek,' said Stark in a low voice. 'It is he that has done this,' and he waved towards the remains of the old man.

'I see,' grunted Dick. 'Midnight must be tonight. Do you know this 'Inn by the River'?'

'Yes, it's a place known only to a few — a smugglers' inn south of here.'

There was a short silence and then Jeremy voiced the thoughts of all of them. 'That, I think, is our next stopping place.'

Said Jonathan Stark: 'It certainly is for me.'

'We're with you, eh Jeremy?' quoth

Palmer, turning to the Squire's son.

'Why, of course, but what of Will Snell?'

'Strike me rigid,' gasped Dick, 'but I had forgotten him!' He faced the newcomer and then, after a moment's thought, told Jonathan Stark in as few words as possible why they sought the gang and of what had happened to his friend Will Snell.

'Another one,' breathed Stark, when Dick had finished, and his lips quivered slightly so that his neat beard twitched.

'Let us return then,' added the newcomer, 'and see if he is right for the road and, if so, we can all ride for the Inn by the River. I avow we will make a staunch band.'

Without more ado the three men mounted their steeds and were soon galloping back along the road to Ewhurst and Mathering Manor.

7

'You have no idea, then, why these rogues have taken your names?' asked Jonathan Stark as they rode along.

'No, it's that problem we hope to solve.'

'I avow it's very strange,' murmured Stark. 'You say there has been some mention of a lady and you saw a woman who seemed familiar at the Monastery Inn?'

'Yes, but I cannot remember where I have seen her before.'

'Maybe we shall find the answer tonight. A female in the case is news to me.'

'What of the fellow, Simon Pendexter?' asked Jeremy.

Jonathan Stark was some time answering; when he did reply he spoke in deep, measured tones: 'As I say I have sought Pendexter this twelve month — he ravished and killed my sister,' he remarked quite unemotionally. 'On top of this, we both seek a certain chart held by one, Jack Cambridge. What with one thing and another — he and I, as you will see, are most unfriendly towards one another!'

Jonathan Stark lapsed into silence, staring thoughtfully ahead, and Jeremy did not pursue the matter. He began to feel sorry for this villain, Simon Pendexter, beast though he seemed, for with Will Snell and the newcomer, who appeared a most powerful character, after his blood he surely had a very short future ahead of him.

'What does this cove look like?' asked Jeremy.

'He is big and mighty strong and, curse him, quite pleasant to look upon. He has a stack of fair hair and a red face, but it's his eyes that give the rogue away They are almost colourless — and watery — as if he's about to break into tears, though that's impossible.' Jonathan Stark smiled grimly and shrugged his shoulders. 'That is Simon Pendexter — don't worry, if you have the misfortune to meet him, then I avow, you will never forget the fellow again.'

They rode on in silence and Dick Palmer suddenly realised that it was nearly noon and that he was hungry. Jeremy Mathering at that moment remarked, as if he had read Dick Palmer's thoughts:

'I'm hungry. It's dinnertime. May I offer you the hospitality of Mathering Manor, Mr. Stark?'

'Why, thank you,' replied the dapper fellow. 'I avow my belly does seem rather empty.'

They cantered up the drive to the manor and all at once the sound of loud, excited voices and running feet reached their ears. 'What goes on?' cried Jeremy fearfully, and he dug in his spurs and galloped ahead.

He came into sight of the house and saw the Squire, black wig awry, standing in the porch staring into space as if he had just seen a ghost; Bob Flint hastening away to the stables; and Will Snell standing in front of the house, waving his arms and bellowing at the top of his voice.

Anxiously Jeremy jumped from his horse and hurried over to his father. 'What's wrong, sir, what's wrong?'

The Squire slowly turned and gazed at Jeremy in a strange vacant manner, but made no reply.

'It's Crimson,' roared Will Snell frantically. 'They've kidnapped her.'

The blood drained from Jeremy Mathering's long face and he stood still. At last he shook himself as if discarding a weighty cloak and strode over to Will Snell.

'Kidnapped her?' he breathed, almost inaudibly. 'Who — who has taken my sister?'

Will calmed down a little and, breathing heavily, explained what had happened. 'Bob Flint was walking in the village with her. Two strangers rode up, sprang upon Crimson, threw her over one horse, and galloped all — before Flint realised what was happening.'

'It must be the same rogues,' cried Dick Palmer.

'But you should have passed them,' exclaimed Will. 'Didn't you meet anyone on the road?'

'Not a soul.'

'Then they will have seen you coming and hidden.'

Jeremy Mathering walked grimly back to his steed and without a word mounted. 'Do you think you are fit enough, Will?' he asked.

'I certainly am,' growled the giant. At that moment he noticed Jonathan Stark and he glared rudely at the newcomer.

Hastily Dick Palmer introduced them and explained the circumstances of their meeting. Jonathan Stark bowed politely. Will Snell bowed back and grunted: 'Good — the more the merrier.'

At this moment Bob Flint appeared, panting, and leading Will's great black stallion. The giant leaped into the saddle with surprising agility, seeming to have completely forgotten his wounded head.

'Are you ready?' he cried.

His companions nodded and immediately they were all galloping furiously down the drive. Out in the village people stared in amazement as the four men thundered off along the road to the Monastery Inn. Gradually Dick Palmer, on his magnificent chestnut mare, took the lead and began to draw away. As he went he shouted back over his shoulder:

'I will try and catch them — see you at the inn.' With that he bent in the saddle and streaked down the highway.

'I avow,' cried Jonathan Stark, astonished, 'that's some steed and some rider.'

The three men lashed their horses to a greater pace and galloped headlong after Dick Palmer. In a short time they came to the brow of the slope leading down to the Monastery Inn and there they saw Red Ruby standing outside, but no Dick Palmer. As they drew nearer Palmer came out of the inn and stood awaiting them.

'The place is empty,' he cried. 'As I rode down the hill the two villains galloped away from the inn towards the south — but there's no Miss Mathering.'

Jeremy cursed, jumped from his horse and drawing his pistol, stepped grimly into the inn. Will Snell followed him and outside the two remaining men could hear their friends noisily searching the premises. In a few minutes Will and Jeremy returned with puzzled frowns on their faces. 'It's true,' cried Will, 'there's not a sign of life.'

Jonathan Stark gazed keenly at the massive door of the inn. 'There's something strange here,' he murmured.

'There is to be sure,' agreed Palmer, 'but there's nothing further we can do. We had better follow the two — maybe they're riding to the Inn by the River.'

Jeremy Mathering hesitated and bit his lip, and Will Snell fingered his beard in a worried fashion, then shrugged his mighty shoulders. 'You're right, Dick, that's the only thing we can do.'

'Let's be off then,' exclaimed Jonathan Stark, 'else we shall lose the trail of these rogues, though I think I know the way to the Pack Horse Inn.'

'The Pack Horse Inn?' queried Will Snell.

'Ah, I forgot to tell you,' replied Stark. 'That's the real name of the inn, though to certain gentlemen of the road and particularly smugglers the place is known as the 'Inn by the River'.'

Jeremy Mathering lingered a moment, glaring about the inn, as if trying to force the secret of his sister's disappearance out of its grey walls. 'She must be somewhere,' he growled. 'If they did not take her away — then she must be here.'

'It's no good, Jeremy,' grunted Will Snell, mounting his horse. 'It's best we follow the two rascals and when we catch 'em — then they'll tell us what they've done with Crimson — with Miss Mathering.'

Jeremy nodded somewhat doubtfully. 'Let us be away then,' and he mounted his horse and a moment later the four men galloped off on the road to the Inn by the River.

8

They rode two abreast, Jonathan Stark and Jeremy Mathering in the lead. There was little time for speech as they galloped swiftly through the undulating countryside, dotted with clumps of tall trees and isolated bushes.

Now and again the four men swept by a countrymen ambling peacefully along the road, and he would jump to one side and stare at them with wide eyes and open mouth. To one such fellow, after they had been travelling a quarter of an hour. Jonathan cried out in his deep voice:

'Ha' you seen two riders pass this way, fine fellow?'

At which the fat fellow stared more and opened his mouth wider, but no words came forth. In a little while they passed a cosy tavern standing in a tiny green dell down which a brook ran merrily to disappear into a steep hill at the far end.

Outside this tavern sat a large man with a great plate before him filled with vast quantities of pork roasted, and he was tucking into this with considerable enthusiasm. Dick Palmer licked his lips and felt a tugging at his stomach. They had not eaten since early morning and it was now well into the afternoon.

Still they raced on, Jonathan Stark watching the horizon ahead for sight of the quarry, but there was no sign of the two men. After a little while he glanced anxiously about him, beginning to doubt they were on the right road. Then abruptly they came upon a crossroads and here Stark held up his hand and the four men came to a halt. He fingered his neat, black beard and then turned in his saddle.

'I avow, but I'm lost.'

Jeremy promptly cursed and stared about him. 'Look, here comes a local lad, let's ask if he has seen ought of the rogues.' Sure enough, strolling towards them from the south was a youth whistling cheerfully as he walked.

When he had reached them Jonathan

Stark asked: 'Pardon me, good sir, but have you seen two horsemen pass you further along the road?'

The youth stopped whistling and fearlessly contemplated the four horsemen. He coughed in an important manner and struck an impressive attitude, highly pleased being called 'good sir.'

''S' matter of fact, I 'ave.'

'Ha — where?'

'Let me see now.' The youth fingered his white chin that boasted two or three long hairs. 'Now I 'ave bin hiking this ten minutes since I sees 'em down yonder road, so I reckon they must 'ave — '

Jonathan Stark waited for no more, but dug in his heels and galloped off closely followed by his companions. They carried on over the crossroads and soon came upon rolling downs, and now they were able to see some distance ahead. The clatter of the horses' hooves travelled far over the countryside and rabbits, suddenly disturbed, raced away across the grass, and birds rose abruptly from their nests and flew squawking into the blue sky above.

'Look yonder,' cried out Stark in a gleeful tone.

On a far hill two tiny figures could be seen against the white ribbon of a road that wound up the hill and disappeared on the horizon. As the four men watched the figures reached the top of the hill and were momentarily silhouetted against the sky. They were two horsemen and were travelling at great speed.

Without a word the four pursuers laid whip to horse and bent in their saddles and thundered after the robbers. A slight gasp from Will Snell made Dick glance at his friend out of the corner of his eye, and he saw that Will's wounds were giving him some trouble, for he rode one hand clapped to the side of his head and a set expression on his face.

Swiftly the four men reached the summit of the hill where they had seen their quarry and ahead was a flat stony stretch of country which appeared rather like a plateau, for the land fell away on all sides. Set in the midst of this rocky plain was a large, solitary building and, even at this distance, the pursuers could make out the name on the board — 'The Pack Horse Inn.' It was a strange, lifeless looking place, seeming like a grim sentinel guarding the high road. There were no other buildings about — just the inn, dark and silent.

Jonathan Stark quickly held up his hand and at once began swinging his horse about, as he cried: 'Back below the ridge, else we'll be seen.'

The four horsemen immediately turned and galloped back and descended the hill a short distance until they were out of sight of the inn. Here they stopped and considered the position. Will Snell lay wearily forward on his black stallion.

'Where's the river?' cried Jeremy.

Jonathan Stark shrugged his slim, broad shoulders. 'Yes, it's strange — I don't know, but I'm certain yonder is what is known as the 'Inn by the River'.' He sat forward in his saddle and folded his arms and gazed at his three companions one by one, his bright, dark eyes keenly studying them He observed, as a consequence, the drooping Will Snell. Then he said: 'What's our plan?'

'First,' replied Dick Palmer, 'I think it would be a good idea to fill our stomachs at that inn we passed, and p'raps snatch forty winks.' With the last words Dick glanced across at Will Snell.

'Just what I was thinking,' agreed Jonathan Stark, also contemplating Will, who sat motionless in his saddle, his chin out of sight in his bristling red beard.

Jeremy grunted: 'Maybe you're right. To be sure I could eat a whole pig. No doubt we can plan our campaign of war with greater facility on full bellies. Follow me, gentlemen, this is on me,' and the Squire's son cantered down the hill.

Upon the appearance of the little tavern in the green dingle, the four men licked their lips appetisingly, rode down to the front of the inn — which went by the name of 'Travellers' Hollow' — and tethered their steeds to a rail fitted around the trunk of a great tree standing close by.

A pretty little girl who could not be more than sixteen appeared at the door with a welcoming smile and called out cheerily: 'And can it be that you gentlemen require a meal and some refreshment?'

'It can be,' replied Jeremy in his lazy drawl, sniffing appreciatively the fragrant aroma that floated out the door of the taproom.

'Then sit down here,' said she, indicating a table beneath a tree at the corner of the inn. 'I think I can satisfy your wants.'

The sun was setting behind the hills in a crimson glow when the four men leaned back from the table with great contented sighs and agreed unanimously that the girl had in effect satisfied their wants most adequately. Will Snell now looked a little better and more full of life as was evidenced by the manner in which he quaffed his ale.

'Feel better, eh?' asked Stark.

Will nodded and grinned. 'I certainly do.'

Stark looked thoughtful and stroked his beard, then suddenly he rose to his feet and entered the inn, and in a moment whispered voices emanated from the taproom. He returned and said to Will:

'Our hostess wishes to speak to you.'

Will Snell stared. 'To me?' he queried.

'Yes — she said most distinctly your good self.'

Will shrugged, finished his ale and then disappeared into the inn. Jonathan Stark, after he had gone, winked mysteriously at Dick and Jeremy and then crossed to the tree and lay down. Within a short while all three had fallen asleep and their gentle snores mingled with a babbling brook a short distance away.

Dick Palmer was awakened by a scuffling sound and he sat up to find that night had come during their sleep and the moon shone down into the dingle giving it a pale ethereal look. Then he saw two figures hurrying away towards the trees on the far side of the dingle and drawing his pistol he fired after them. Immediately Jeremy and Jonathan were awake and Will Snell appeared at the inn door. Palmer's shot went wide and a minute later the sound of hooves upon the other side of the trees was heard, then two horsemen appeared on the skyline some three hundred paces away and in a moment they had gone.

Jonathan Stark was staring down at the grass near where Palmer had been lying. 'I avow,' said he, 'it's strange — these marauders have been close to you, Dick, but they never touched you.'

Dick looked at the grass where Jonathan pointed and saw that in two places leading to the brook it had been trampled down. 'Yes, it's as I say, Jonathan, they use our names, yet don't try to kill us.'

'I'm convinced,' Dick remarked quietly, reaching for his hat, 'they wish to capture Will and I for some reason, and that reason, I'm sure, concerns this woman I have seen at the Monastery Inn.'

The moonlight played on Jonathan Stark's dark aquiline features accentuating their sharpness as he nodded thoughtfully at Dick Palmer's words. Jeremy turned to Will Snell who had just joined them. 'Well, Will, an' you look mighty refreshed — do I see a clean bandage around that massive top-knot of yours?'

'You do, Jeremy, and I am feeling much better after my sleep. The young miss very kindly tended to my wounds and she says they are healing fine.'

'You know, Dick, if I had been you,' said Jonathan Stark suddenly, 'and these coves were Simon Pendexter then I would be laid out there now like a squashed beetle.'

'Did you see these fellows?' asked Will of Dick.

Palmer shook his head. 'No, but it's certain that they came from that doleful inn on yonder plain, and so we can take it that Pendexter and his band know of our whereabouts.'

'When do we make a move?' asked Jeremy, laying his long frame down on one of the nearby chairs.

'I reckon,' suggested Stark, 'that we wait 'till near midnight. It's then that they meet according to the note. An' then two of us can go forward and chance our luck.'

'Agreed,' said Will heartily. 'So we have at least two hours drinking time,.'

They all returned to the table. 'Agnes,'

bellowed Will, and there was a rustle of petticoats as the pretty young lady came running out. 'Agnes,' said Will 'we require more ale — we shall be here longer than we thought.'

'I am pleased to hear it,' she replied, 'and how is your wound, Will?'

'Much better, Agnes, much better, but how else could it be after such expert and tender attention?' At this the girl blushed and hurried inside. She reappeared in a moment balancing a tray loaded with any number of tankards of foaming ale.

'There,' she gasped. 'I hope they last you 'till you are gone, but if not my father will attend to your wants, I must be off to bed now.'

'Oh, I'm sorry to hear it, but a bonny night to you my beautiful nurse,' cried Will effusively, 'many thanks for your sweet and considerate attention — may your dreams be as lovely as you yourself!'

This went down very well with Agnes and, blushing a great deal more, she curtsied shyly and ran daintily back into the inn. Dick Palmer grinned and shook his head. 'Nay, Will, she will be dreaming of you, I reckon, and your gallant ways!'

'So be it,' exclaimed Will and he picked up one of the tankards and took a long, copious draught. He turned then to Jonathan Stark.

'Now, Jonathan, let us hear about this cove Simon Pendexter — he who did this,' and Will pointed grimly at his bandaged head.

Jonathan Stark nodded. 'Yes, I'll tell you,' he said quietly, a fiery gleam entering his dark eyes. He lifted his tankard and drank well, then he replaced it and leaned forward, glancing at his listeners.

9

A peaceful serenity reigned in the little moonlit dell and the four men sat in comparative darkness except for the odd shaft of moonlight that penetrated the foliage of the tree above. The inn, close by, was black and silent and the whole world seemed to have come to a breathless halt as Jonathan Stark, in his deep, low tones, commenced his story.

'My home was at the foot of the Cotswolds near Gloucester. I had a sister by the name of Anne,' Jonathan Stark's neat beard twitched as he mentioned the last word. 'One night we attended a dance in the village and it was nearly midnight when four strangers entered. They were a rough looking crowd and one was a great, blonde cove who carried himself with a confident air.'

Jonathan took a sip of his ale and replaced the tankard carefully on the table. 'He strolled across to Anne and requested the next dance and she, of course, delighted, accepted and away they went. I avow,' said Stark grimly, 'it was at that very moment that I took a dislike to the fellow. It was his eyes — they were watery and colourless. Never have I seen such eyes.

'I was in the middle of a dance myself when it came to me that Anne and this newcomer had vanished. I grew worried, but I could not investigate immediately, for I must needs pay attention to my chattering partner.

'The dance was nearly finished when there was a commotion at the door and two men I knew came rushing in. 'Jonathan,' they shouted, 'Jonathan.' Something was amiss — that I could well see by their expressions — and a terrible coldness came upon me. I left my partner and hurried over to them.

''It's your sister, Anne,' they gasped, 'come outside.'

'I followed them and they led me to Anne, who lay beneath a bush a short distance from the hall.' Jonathan Stark's lips parted in a mirthless grin as he stared round at his three companions; there was a wild, frightened look in his eyes. 'She had been murdered,' he whispered.

'As I stared upon her there came the sound of hooves and suddenly a horseman galloped by heading for the hills. I recognised the fair man who had danced with Anne, and at once I raced away for my own steed and gave chase.

'Now my horse then was the fastest in the county, a really fine courser, being a present from my father. I caught up with this fellow on the tops of the Cotswolds. I remember there was a strong wind blowing and in the moonlight I could see his fair locks billowing out, like a pennant, behind him. I leaped straight upon him and we fell to the ground in grim combat and we fought furiously with our bare fists.'

Jonathan Stark suddenly smiled. 'Ah, but I think have you interested, eh?' he asked.

'You certainly have,' cried Jeremy, 'carry on.'

'By a trick,' continued Stark, 'he threw me from him, though I don't think I could have held him much longer for he was mighty strong, and then he leaped for his steed. I thought he intended to make his escape so jumped for his bridle. But I was mistaken — and thus I first made the acquaintance of the spiked boy.'

Will Snell leaned nearer at these words.

'He drew something from a leather sheath hanging from his saddle and swung it about his head, and I could see it clear against the sky. It was an iron ball some four inches across, and all over there protruded divers sharp spikes — this wicked thing was attached to the end of a thick thong with which he twirled the weapon about him.'

'Ah-h,' murmured Will, in a long drawn-out breath.

'I leaped to one side in a vain effort to escape the blow aimed at my face, but he caught my shoulder and I fell dizzily to the ground. Not waiting to see the result of his attack he ran to his horse and in a moment galloped off. By the time I had regained my feet he was gone.'

'Well, well,' exclaimed Palmer, leaning back in his seat and staring wonderingly at Stark. 'Have you seen him since?'

'Yes — twice. Once in London town and once on the Kentish coast, but they're other stories and, as you know, the fiend is still at large.'

'I think,' announced Jeremy, 'the sooner we get after him the better it will be for my sister, Crimson.' He rose, an anxious look upon his long face. 'Come, to our steeds.'

Jonathan Stark nodded. 'Yes, let us be off.' He added: 'You will understand now, my friends, why I seek Simon Pendexter.'

'I understand,' replied Will, 'but I reckon we all seek him now, for it's certain he is connected with the abduction of Miss Mathering. On top o' that,' said Will, tapping his bandage, 'I also have something to repay the rogue for.'

The four men strode over to their horses and in a moment were trotting up the road towards the Pack Horse Inn. Reaching the edge of the rocky plain they halted and watched the dark building for any sign of life. It was a clear, moonlit night and an opalescent light lay over the scene so that the inn and the bushes and rocks dotted about the plain were brought out in sharp relief. No lamp glowed from the inn windows and the place appeared deserted.

Jonathan Stark turned to his companions, his dark features indistinct but for the glitter in his eyes and the paleness of his skin. 'Two of us should venture forward first. Who will accompany me?'

'I will,' replied Jeremy.

'Good.' Stark turned to Will Snell. 'Now Will, if we do not return before — let me see — before the moon is over yonder big rock, then you and Dick may take whatever action you think best.'

Will Snell nodded, and then Jonathan Stark galloped forward towards the Pack Horse Inn closely followed by Jeremy Mathering. The rock Stark had indicated lay over to their right and Palmer calculated it would take the moon perhaps half an hour to reach that position.

They watched the two men pass swiftly over the plain and in a short while Jonathan and Jeremy disappeared as they came within the shadow of the inn.

However straining their eyes the watchers could faintly discern their figures as they dismounted and approached the house. They appeared to be creeping along the wall silently seeking an entrance, and then quite suddenly they vanished, and try as they would Dick and Will could see them no more.

'Ha,' grunted Will, 'they've got inside.'

Silence followed as the two friends sat motionless on their steeds a little above the plain so that they could watch without themselves being seen. Now and again they glanced at the big rock out on the plain and very slowly the moon drew nearer to it.

Still the two men said nothing, but watched the inn grimly, wondering what was taking place behind its forbidding walls. The moon continued on its ordained path and now approached the position above the rock. Dick Palmer's restless anxiety was conveyed to his mare Red Ruby, for she abruptly took several steps forward on to the plain tossing her head impatiently. Cursing beneath his breath he pulled hard on the reins and slowly forced her back into line again. He glanced across the plain for the sixth time and saw that the moon was now directly over the bog rock.

'It's time, Dick,' whispered Will Snell. 'They can see us on our steeds, so we cannot ride up. But if we go round the edge of the plain and come up behind yonder big rock, they won't see us. We'll tether our horses behind the rock, and then creep forward on hands and knees. We should escape notice altogether amongst the shadows of the bushes and rocks.'

'Right — perhaps we shall surprise them.'

★ ★ ★

Jonathan Stark and Jeremy Mathering, upon arrival in the deep shadow cast by the Pack Horse Inn, dismounted silently and tethered their horses to a rail in front of the inn. The two men stole forward to one of the windows and stood several moments listening, but not a sound reached their ears. Very carefully, Jeremy edged forward and looked in through the window. Inside he could faintly discern the dark objects that were tables and chairs, and tiny glittering lights that were the reflections from the glasses and bottles. Except for these things the room appeared empty.

With pistol in hand Jonathan Stark tried the handle of the door. He turned it and pushed slightly and the door opened. Stark looked at his young friend in surprise. Whatever was the door doing open at this time of the night? Stark became suspicious and the two men grew doubly cautious. The door was now half open; it was too late to turn back. With beating hearts they moved slowly forward through the doorway and into the room, straining their eyes trying to see into the furthermost corners. Stark, his short black beard jutting forward like the bows of a ship, stepped to the centre the room and looked about him. A deep almost unnatural silence lay upon the inn and about the place lingered a musty smell and a deserted air.

To the left of the bar was the black

opening to a passage and Jonathan Stark flitted over the floor and peered down the passage like a bird of prey. It was as the two men entered this opening they each felt a numbing blow upon the crown of the head and the darkness around them all of a sudden became complete blackness.

It seemed to Jeremy that it was but a few seconds later that he opened his eyes again, to hear the sound of lapping water. He tried to move and found that he was trussed like a chicken, and then his senses returned completely and he stared about him. Just ahead all bound securely, was Jonathan Stark, and they lay upon the narrow bank of an underground river.

The sound of shouts and cries reached them and now and then a rough-looking seafaring fellow appeared down some stone steps farther along and threw some objects into one of two large row-boats moored nearby, Jonathan Stark wormed himself alongside Jeremy and whispered:

'We're fools!'

'Why?'

'To have walked into such a simple trap.'

'Yes, p'raps we were, but what now?'

'They seem to be loading up,' whispered Jonathan. 'They'll be off in the boat somewhere before long.'

Hardly had Stark spoken these words than half a score of men came tumbling down the steps and piled into the boat; then there followed slow, heavy footsteps and Jonathan Stark suddenly tensed and his little beard bristled like the hairs of a cat.

Down the steps there appeared a great man, broad of shoulder, mighty of chest and red of face. With a start Jeremy noticed by the light of the lantern the fellow carried that his curly and unruly hair was as fair as a woman's. He came along the bank towards them smiling quite pleasantly. And Jeremy, glancing out of the corner of his eye at Jonathan Stark, saw his friend taut like a bowstring.

The giant halted before them and his smile broadened and he cried in a surprisingly high voice: 'Well, if it ain't me old friend Jonathan. Well, well, well!'

Simon Pendexter swung the lantern down so that he could look at his prisoners the better, and as he did so the light shone in his eyes and Jeremy Mathering felt his stomach turn over. The giant's eyes were a pale yellow colour and they had a strange, sightless appearance.

'I must admit, Jonathan dear fellow, I never thought I'd take you as easily as this.'

Stark glared back at him, his head jutting forward like a hound's straining at the leash, but he did not reply. Pendexter turned benignly to Jeremy.

'And I believe you're Mathering?'

'Yes, I am,' cried Jeremy, 'and where have you got my sister, you fiend?'

'Why at Toby-Joy — at Toby-Joy. But come, we are wasting time,' said Pendexter. 'Snapper — Ben, pick up these fools and throw them aboard; we have no time to waste.'

At his command two big men jumped out of the boat and ran along the bank They lifted the two prisoners and half carrying, half dragging them, brought them to the side of the row-boat and then tipped them unceremoniously into the stern. At this action there were loud guffaws from the men and a number of coarse remarks at the prisoners' expense.

'Quieten your tongues,' cried Simon Pendexter, stepping aboard, 'an' cast off else we shall miss the ship.'

Immediately the motley crew was silent, the rope was unhitched and the men bent to the oars and the rowboat shot off downstream. The tunnel was pitch black except for the light from the lantern, and Simon Pendexter held this aloft in the bows and directed the man at the rudder, whose name appeared to be Ned.

Jeremy and Jonathan lay in the bottom of the boat near the man called Ned, who was continually yawning, and their thoughts were most dismal. One fact, however, to a certain degree cheered up Jeremy: it seemed that Crimson was held at Toby-Joy to await the return of these rogues, so at least she was as yet unharmed.

'I avow, Jeremy,' muttered Stark, 'we're

131

in a fine pickle. How do we escape from this?'

'Maybe Will and Dick will follow us,' replied Jeremy hopefully.

Jonathan Stark set his lips grimly and shrugged. 'Let's hope so but how they'll save us from whatever this creature has in store for us I'm afraid I cannot see.'

'Ha, ha, me hearties,' cried the man at the rudder. ' 'Fraid you going to be dis'pointed; there's four fine mates o' mine back at the inn awaiting 'em. The Lady requires them two special like.'

To this the prisoners made no comment and stared up at the roof of the tunnel with despair eating at their hearts. Nevertheless Jonathan Stark tried hard to think of some way out of their present situation, impossible though it seemed. He dare not dwell on the terrible entertainment that Simon Pendexter would undoubtedly arrange as a preliminary to their death.

So they traversed the underground river to the steady rhythmic splash of the oars and the curt orders of Simon Pendexter. Suddenly the orange glow given out by the lantern was greatly strengthened by a pale, opaque light and the pitch blackness about them disappeared and there was a scraping and brushing along the side of the boat.

The black roof now gave place to one that had a purple tint and which was sprinkled with a myriad twinkling lights. The two prisoners in the bottom the boat thus knew they had joined the main river as in a moment the boat began to dip and roll uncomfortably. Heaving himself up, Jeremy glanced over the side and could faintly discern the tree-lined banks.

'Now me lubbers,' cried Pendexter in his high-pitched voice, 'bend to your oars an' let's be moving.'

Immediately the rowboat sprang forward as the men obeyed his command and Jonathan and Jeremy rolled about in the bottom like sacks of corn. The little man at the rudder began singing a lewd song of the seas but such was his yawning that the effort became a most disjointed affair.

'Nay, Nodding Ned,' cried Pendexter, 'make up your mind, one or t'other; you can't sing and yawn at the same time.'

To this the man at the rudder, who Jeremy observed had an almighty large head for one of his size, gave a long final yawn and relapsed into silence. A moment later Simon Pendexter suddenly spat out a lurid oath.

'You're a lazy crew,' he screamed. 'More speed else we won't make it.'

'Simon,' said the man at the rudder, 'we're over-weighted — we 'ave some useless cargo aboard.'

'I see what you mean, Ned,' grunted Pendexter thoughtfully; 'it's a shame for I would have liked a little sport with our friends there.'

The man at the rudder nodded his great round head so that his thin lank hair shook like the plaits of a mop. 'It certainly is a mighty big shame, Simon. I had already thought of two new ways of entertaining ourselves with 'em.'

Simon Pendexter rose from the bow of the boat and clambered back towards his prisoners. He halted above them and grinned down amiably, and then Jeremy saw that he was twirling some object around his hand — something that glittered in the moonlight.

Pendexter squatted down at the side of Jonathan Stark, twirling the spiked boy with great dexterity so that the sharp spikes came near to touching Jonathan's nose. The captive's face turned deathly pale but otherwise no other outward indication did he give of his fear; the hideous weapon. There was a strange, greedy glare in Pendexter's eyes and Jeremy only just withheld a cold shudder.

Nodding Ned at the rudder licked his lips and watched with hypnotic fascination.

'Jonathan, me dear friend,' whispered the giant in his squeaky voice, 'it has always been my devout wish that I may some day remove that sharp nose of yours.'

Very slowly Simon Pendexter lowered the arc of the whirling boy and Jeremy found his eyes caught by the glittering circle it made. Then something snapped in his brain and all at once he shouted:

'Overboard with you, Jonathan, overboard for God's sake; it's a better way!'

With this cry Jeremy Mathering managed somehow to raise his lanky frame on to his knees, bound hand and foot though he was, and he flung himself against Simon Pendexter. The giant sprawled backwards against one of the rowers and before a hand could stay them, both prisoners had half rolled and half tumbled over the side of the boat into the swirling waters of the river.

Jeremy instinctively took a deep breath before he hit the water, though he knew the futility of it, and then both men sank like stones to the bed of the river. Above, Simon Pendexter began cursing but abruptly he stopped and instead gave out a great roar of laughter that floated far over the waters.

* * *

Dick Palmer and Will Snell rode along beneath the edge of the plateau hidden from view of the inn. When they had reached a point where the big rock was between them and their objective they spurred up and galloped swiftly over the plain. They quickly reached the sanctuary of the large black rock and dismounted. Will searched about for some suitable outjutting of rock and, finding one, they tethered their horses to it securely. From the rock the inn was some two hundred paces away, and thus it was necessary that they crawl over the rough, broken ground for that distance. It was an unpleasant task and the two men surveyed the sharp stones and rocks with grim expressions. But Will glanced at his young friend to see if he were ready, and upon his nod the great fellow dropped on to his stomach and they commenced their weird journey.

There was little likelihood, though the moon still shone brightly that they would be seen, for the scattered bushes and rocks provided excellent cover and cast many shadows, so that a great part of the surface of the plain was in darkness.

At last, after an interminable time it seemed, with great gasps and heavy panting, the two men collapsed beneath one of the inn walls and they lay there to regain their breath and to inspect the divers cuts and bruises they had received on the long crawl from the rock It was as they were lying thus that whispered voices reached their ears and the words, which came from the taproom of the inn, went thus:

'What do you think they're up to?' said one voice.

'Nay, I don't know. They were over beyond the plain but now gawd knows where they are,' said another

'I don't like this sitting in the dark,' grunted a third.

'Ha! Stop quavering,' muttered a fourth fiercely; 'we're as safe as a man o'war 'ere behind the bar.'

Will Snell turned swiftly to Palmer: 'Did you hear that?' he whispered in an exultant tone. Dick nodded:

'Yes, if we can come up behind 'em we should have the coves.'

'Let us crawl around to the back of the inn,' Will whispered, 'an' see if we can get in somewhere there.' With that he slid off like a great snake and in a few moments they had reached the rear of the building. Here they remained silent and still for a second or two and then Will slowly got to his feet and tried the back door of the inn. It was locked. Dick Palmer, however, was more successful for, quietly fiddling away at one of the windows, he suddenly got his finger in a slit and very gently was able to slide it open.

Beckoning to Will, he clambered through and found himself in the kitchen behind the taproom. A door on each side of the kitchen led into the bar and almost immediately Palmer had thought of a scheme by which he and Will could surprise the four men within. In a whisper he outlined his idea to Will and that worthy nodded and murmured: 'We can but try, Dick.'

Thereupon the two men began searching for a lantern and in a few minutes Will discovered one beneath the sink. He handed it to Palmer and the latter lit it with his tinderbox and turned the lantern down low. They parted and each went and stood by one of the doors leading into the taproom. Will clasped a pistol in each hand and Dick the lantern in one, a pistol in the other. They waited in silence for a short while and then Will raised his hand and they both abruptly burst open the doors and leaped forward into the taproom.

As they had conjectured, they found themselves at each end of the bar, and between them and behind the bar crouched the four men, who gaped at them in dumbfounded amazement.

'Avast!' roared Will. 'Make a move and you die!'

Quickly Dick Palmer laid the lantern on the bar table and turned up the wick, then he drew his second pistol. So they confronted the four bewildered men.

'Now, my fair scoundrels,' cried Will threateningly, 'throw your weapons at my feet.'

With a highly offended air the four men did as they requested and then sat sullenly awaiting his next order. Will relaxed a little and grinned across at Palmer, and both felt delighted with the simple success of the plan.

'Find a rope, Dick, an' tie 'em up; I can take care of the rogues whilst you're away.'

Palmer pocketed his pistols and re-entered

the kitchen. In a little while he returned with a length of stout cord. With this he began tying up their prisoners, one to the other, in a most secure fashion, and when he had finished he stepped back to survey his handiwork.

Will Snell lowered his pistols. 'An excellent piece of work. I swear I have never seen a prettier bunch o' cut-throats.'

The four prisoners lay in an ungainly heap behind the bar scowling and muttering various pleasantries, and indeed they were a rough-looking crew. One wore a black patch over one eye, another had only one ear and a third sported a great scar from the top of his forehead to his bearded chin. The fourth, a small, wicked looking fellow, appeared to be unblemished.

To the one-eared gentleman Will presented a pistol, pointing it directly at the fellow's remaining ear. 'What think you, Dick, to blowing this cove's other ear off?'

Dick Palmer looked somewhat surprised. Hardly fair. He had not thought his big friend capable of such an act. After all, the fellow wouldn't then have any at all! The one-eared captive promptly screamed and wailed: 'Nay, nay, master, not that, I crave of you — it be me only one — anything but that.'

Will's blue eyes gleamed: 'Tell me, then,' he growled, 'where have your comrades taken the two men before us?'

'Why,' cried the one-eared man, 'on the row-boat down the river to Littlehampton.'

'River!' cried Will. 'River — where — what river?'

'It's underground,' replied the one-eared man, giving a sigh of relief as Will withdrew the pistol slightly. 'The steps be at the end of yonder passage.'

10

Will Snell glanced across at Palmer. 'That's the next step I fancy, Dick.'

The younger man nodded but as they hurried towards the passage he halted and stared back at the doleful looking bunch of rogues. 'Tell me, One Ear' he exclaimed, 'what is Toby-Joy, and who be the Lady?'

One Ear's round face blanched and he gave a low gasp of fear. 'Nay, master, that I dare not answer, it's more than me life. Pendexter would rip me apart — strewth he would.'

'Well, then,' said Dick Palmer patiently, 'can you tell me why this lady seeks us?'

'Aye, I can answer that,' replied One Ear. 'I don't know.'

Will Snell grunted. 'It's no use, Dick; let us be off. We shall find the solution no doubt before many an hour has passed.'

Palmer hesitated and then shrugged his shoulders. 'You're right, Will; lead on. We have no time to waste bandying words with that scum.'

They ran down the passage, Dick holding the lantern aloft to light the way. They reached the end of the passage and here they found stone steps that led down abruptly into pitch darkness, and out of the depths of this abyss there arose the faint sound of the lapping of water. Gingerly the two men descended the steps, straining their eyes trying to see into the darkness beyond the circle of light from the lantern. At last they came to the water's edge and they stared down with some aversion at the ugly, black, slow-moving mass.

'So,' breathed Dick, 'this is why it is known as the 'Inn by the River'.'

'Most useful for a bit of smuggling.'

Suddenly Palmer raised his hand: 'Hark, Will, do you hear that?'

They both remained very still and listened and at first Will could hear nothing but the lapping of the water, which appeared to have a strange, depressing and ominous note to it, then faintly the sound of a man's voice reached his ears.

'It's fading,' whispered Dick. 'I swear it's their boat. Come on, we'll take this one.'

Without more ado they leaped into the second rowboat, which was tied up at the bottom of the steps. Will grabbed the oars and bent his mighty back and in a moment the boat shot forward along the tunnel with Dick Palmer standing in the bows with the lantern guiding it on the right course.

Their progress was slow, for Will was unable to row at any great speed because of the danger of dashing the flimsy craft against the solid rock sides of the tunnel. Knowing, however, that speed was essential if they wished to save their two friends, their slow movement was particularly frustrating, and Will began to grow impatient.

'Nay, Dick, can you not see the outlet yet?'

'No, Will, this river seems never to end.'

Muttering curses, Will rowed on, carefully feeling his way under Palmer's directions, and the giant swore the more when they suddenly found themselves bumping up against the black rock sides of the tunnel. They swung free and almost at once Dick gave a triumphant cry.

'Ahead, Will — ahead! It's the outlet!'

Will Snell grunted and espying now a grey circular patch in the far distance he bent grimly to the oars and the boat bore swiftly down upon the outlet.

'Easy, Will, easy; they may not be far ahead.'

Gently the rowboat nosed itself through the tangle of bushes at the outlet and Palmer turned the lantern out and crouched down as they reached the main river. Glancing downstream they at once spotted the black shape of the smugglers' boat some four hundred yards away in the middle of the river. The moon shone brightly so that the pursuers could just make out the figures in the boat. Will guided their vessel close into the bank and made as much speed as possible.

'Dick,' he growled, 'we cannot keep up with them, there must be eight or ten rowers in yonder boat.'

Palmer joined Will Snell at the oars and at once they made good headway but all the time they saw, with consternation, the boat ahead swiftly growing smaller. It was thus that, with glancing over their shoulders every few moments towards the smugglers' boat they saw a large man suddenly start walking back in the direction of the stern. Reaching this point the figure crouched down and appeared to be doing something in the bottom.

Will and Dick abruptly stopped rowing and stared keenly ahead, for now the sound of a man's voice floated across the water to them.

'Look!' gasped Dick Palmer.

Without warning from out of the bowels of the distant boat two lengthy bundles appeared to leap up and in a moment had disappeared over the side, and the splash was seen clearly by the two men in the following boat. There came a loud guffaw and the boat continued on its way and in a short while had passed out of sight round a bend in the river.

'It's them I swear!' cried Dick. 'Quick, Will, row like the devil whilst I keep my peepers pinned on the spot.'

As their rowboat left the sanctuary of

the riverbank and shot out towards the place where the two bundles had disappeared into the water, Palmer began divesting himself of his boots and top clothing, at the same time keeping his eyes on their objective. He drew his knife, the long thin blade glinting in the moonlight, and stepped into the bow of the boat.

He stared down into the rushing waters and suddenly waved his arm and Will at once rowed in reverse with all his strength, and the boat came to a bobbing standstill. Then Dick Palmer dived, his knife between his teeth, and he shot down through the sparkling water. Will gazed anxiously over the edge and after some time he was able to make out faint, blurred objects moving around near the bed of the river, but what was happening down there he could not tell. Bubbles came to the surface and Will grew worried and he threw off his boots prepared to dive himself and risk the boat floating away on the swift current.

Then he saw that one of the shapeless objects was rising and in a moment as it neared the surface he realised that it was Jeremy Mathering. Will leaned over the side and as Jeremy's head broke the surface he reached out and heaved him into the boat, the while Jeremy took great gulps of air one after the other. Another blurred bundle rose to the surface and it was Jonathan Stark. Dick Palmer broke the water by his side and Will helped them both safely into the craft.

Will sat and watched them as all three panted, gulped and gasped like fish out of water. At last Jonathan Stark smoothed his short beard and tried to get it back into its former neat shape. Then he gazed at Will and slowly a large, expansive grin spread over his sharp features. His teeth showed white and his watery eyes sparkled, and he grinned more and more.

Will smiled back. 'How are you?' he asked.

'Fine!' gasped Stark. 'Fine, thank you.' Then he added: 'I thought Simon Pendexter had won after all!' He laughed. 'Nay, but he'll be mighty surprised to see me again!'

Jeremy was smiling too, and in his eyes

there was a look of great relief, for it had been an unpleasant experience. 'Thank you, Dick, thank you a thousand times. I thought it was the end.' The Squire's son presented a sorry picture with his soaking clothes clinging to his long frame and his wet hair plastered to the sides of his head.

Will Snell began to pull for the land. 'We had better find an inn where you can dry out,' he observed.

The three men had now begun shivering, for it was cool on the river at nighttime. However, they soon reached the bank and they jumped out and swung their arms about to keep warm.

'Let us hope there's an inn hereabouts,' grunted Dick as they clambered up the steep bank, 'else we shall take the plague.'

A lane ran close by parallel to the river, and along this the four men tramped. After they had travelled some distance without a sign of an inn they all grew despondent, and their depression increased as each bend in the lane revealed still more trees and bushes without a single break.

The three men who had been in the water were now shivering with some energy and the sound of their footsteps was accompanied by the sound of their chattering teeth. The moon had now passed behind some cloud and with the high trees on each side the lane was dark and lonely, and the comrades straggled along slowly and forlornly.

As they walked along a straight stretch of the lane Jeremy happened to glance at the trees on his right and thereupon he gave a sudden cry of delight. 'Look!' he shouted.

At once they all looked in the direction of his pointing finger and there espied a tiny inn nestling deep in the wood, as if trying to hide itself from travellers on the highway. A narrow winding path led up to its dark, frowning façade.

'Ha!' cried Jonathan, 'at last. Come, let us wake the landlord and see what he can provide.'

With lighter steps and cheerful countenances the four men hurried along the path, gazing expectantly forward at the tiny inn. A broken down signpost announced that the place was named the 'Jocular Jack'.

Not bothering with the incongruity of the title, Will Snell rapped loudly on the door and in a little while there came sounds of movement upstairs. Will knocked again and a silence followed. Then a window above them was flung open and an angry, bald head appeared and glared furiously down at the four dishevelled travellers.

'What in God's name is this?' roared the bald head, 'awaking me up at this time o' the night. Away with you, rogues.'

Will Snell realised that the situation would have to be handled with considerable tact. 'Oh, good landlord,' cried he, 'please can you not help four poor unfortunate travellers who have this day been attacked and thrown in yonder chilly river?'

The landlord of the Jocular Jack continued to glare furiously, surveying the men below with great suspicion. 'How do I know you aren't footpads and this not a crafty ruse to rob me?'

'You don't, oh kind landlord, for how can we show that we are not?' replied Will. 'But this I say: you shall be well repaid if you'll let us enter and dry our clothes and sleep till morning.'

Abruptly the bald head disappeared and the four men waited hopefully outside the door. In a moment they saw a flickering candle within the house and then the door was half opened and the bald head peeped out somewhat affrightedly.

'Ah!' cried Will, 'it's indeed most kind of you, landlord,' and with that he pushed open the door wider and stepped inside followed by his three dripping companions.

The landlord still eyed them suspiciously, but trade had been bad and he could not pass by this chance of good remuneration. He let them walk into the small parlour at the back of the inn, where a smouldering fire soon leaped into warm flames upon the energetic prodding of a poker in the chilly hands of Jonathan Stark.

Will licked his lips. 'Oh for a lovely cup of tea,' said he, as if speaking to himself.

The landlord grunted and went off in his nightclothes to the kitchen and there began boiling a kettle. Not long after they were all drinking with great relish steaming mugs of tea, and the landlord had unbent to such an extent that he was chatting away cheerfully as if he was used to receiving four strangers of a bedraggled appearance at his inn in the middle of the night.

'Ah! That was most excellent,' commented Stark thoughtfully staring into his empty mug. Then he glanced up at the landlord. 'Have you room for all of us to stay the night?'

'Yes, I have — two rooms with two beds in each.'

'Good,' grunted Jonathan, 'then the sooner I get out of these wet clothes the better.' He turned to the other three: 'Are you gentlemen ready?'

Jeremy gave a mighty yawn. 'I am,' he replied. 'Let's sleep and then on the morrow seek my sister with redoubled energy.'

'I'll show you the way, sirs, and I hope that you'll be comfortable.'

'Quite sure we will,' exclaimed Will, and the four men followed mine host up the narrow staircase to the tiny, low-ceilinged rooms above. Soon silence had settled down in the Jocular Jack and the four men slept heavily and peacefully.

11

It was following breakfast the next morning that the three men sat outside the Jocular Jack discussing their next move on the road to Toby-Joy. Jeremy Mathering and Will Snell were for returning to the Monastery Inn and prevailing forcefully upon the bar man to reveal the whereabouts of Crimson Mathering. Dick Palmer and Jonathan Stark, however, pointed out that they had no horses and that they had best return to the Pack Horse Inn and collect them and then await the return of Simon Pendexter and his men. Upon the latter's arrival they could follow the gang and thus learn the meaning of Toby-Joy and no doubt release Crimson Mathering at the same time.

'Ha! I was forgetting we have no steeds,' grunted Will. 'You're right; we can't walk to the Monastery Inn, that's certain.'

'Maybe we can hire horses,' suggested Jeremy.

'From where?' enquired Palmer. 'There's none here.'

'Then how do we reach the Pack Horse Inn? I cant swim yonder river.'

'Nay, there must be a bridge somewhere,' said Stark, fingering his short beard. 'Let's ask the landlord, then we can be off. I'm dying to avenge my dip in the river with Pendexter.' He fingered his beard again and gazed off into the trees in a distant manner and added thoughtfully: 'Yes, that's one more reason.'

'It's agreed, then,' cried Will. 'An' I must admit I will be glad to lay me own hands upon this fellow Pendexter,' and the giant tenderly felt his bandages, which were now sadly awry and very soiled looking.

Seeing this movement Dick Palmer exclaimed: 'Why, I had almost forgotten your wounds, Will; you have not said much. How are they?'

'Healing well, I think, thanks Dick, for I don't feel them 'cept for a slight throbbing.'

Jonathan Stark rose from the table. 'I'll ask the landlord the best route to the Pack Horse Inn.' He had but taken two steps towards the door when he halted and turned round and quietly returned to his seat. Three horsemen had reined in their steeds out on the highway and were staring towards the inn. They consulted with one another for several moments and then they swung their horses round and came galloping up the path. They dismounted near to the seated four and tethered their steeds to a rail.

'Top o' the mornin' to you,' trilled one, a fat, oily looking creature, dark of complexion and, by his appearance, dark of nature.

' 'Mornin' to you,' replied Stark, eyeing them speculatively.

The other two men, one a large hairy fellow and the second a small, shifty character, followed the fat man into the inn. In a moment the fat man could be heard ordering the drinks and these were his words:

' 'Mornin', landlord. You're honoured this morn with great company. Three tankards of ale — one for meself, one for the famous highwayman Dick Palmer here, and one for his friend, Will Snell.'

The four listeners outside sat bolt upright in their seats and stared in blank amazement at one another.

'It's them,' breathed Will, rising from his seat and delving in his capacious coat pocket.

'Stay,' whispered Stark, raising one hand, 'let's listen awhile; maybe we'll hear news to our benefit.'

Will Snell nodded and sat down again and all four remained very still and cocked their ears to the open window above them.

'How much further is it, Pedro, to Toby-Joy?'

'Why, but twenty kilometres, Will,' replied the oily man.

Outside Jeremy whispered: 'Pedro! But that's Spanish, yet he speaks good English.'

'Born in this country, no doubt,' replied Will quickly. Inside the conversation continued as follows:

'And you say there's plenty of drink, heh?'

'Everything you want, Will.'

'Ha! That's good. The lady said as I would like the place.'

'Yes, and she has a real treat on for this very night. She has sent two fellows away to London not an hour ago, so I hear, to fetch — to fetch your wife, Dick.'

'My wife?' came the voice of the shifty person, 'but I ain't married.'

'I know you ain't, you fool. I mean Dick Palmer's wife — the fellow you're supposed to be.'

Outside Palmer's young face went as white as the paint on the window-sill and slowly he rose, staring at his companions with blue eyes full of fear and horror; he drew both his pistols and stepped forward to the door.

'Now for it!' muttered Will, glancing at Jeremy and Jonathan, and he also got to his feet.

The three newcomers were standing at the bar with their backs to the door when the four men entered. They did not observe Dick Palmer until he was nearly halfway across the room, then they swung about and stared in surprise at the grim young man who advanced upon them with two pistols levelled menacingly.

'Holy snakes!' cried the big hairy fellow 'And what's all this?'

Dick Palmer halted before them and considered them silently, then he said in a low, threatening voice: 'Say again, cursed fiend, that about the wife of Dick Palmer.'

The oily fat fellow named Pedro raised his eyebrows, which were almost non-existent, and replied: 'Why pal, what's the alarm? It's only that two friends of mine have gone to visit her.'

'I am Dick Palmer,' said Dick between clenched teeth.

At this there was much consternation amongst the three and a wary look came into the bright eyes of Pedro. There was a short silence as the men digested the information.

Palmer levelled one pistol at Pedro's fat stomach and it was quite obvious by the look in his eyes that he would use the weapon without a second thought. 'How long ago did they set off?' he asked.

''Bout an hour,' grunted Pedro, realising that the four men meant business.

'Who sent them?'

'The lady.'

'And who's she?'

Pedro hesitated, then replied: 'I don't know 'cept that she owns the Monastery Inn.'

'Landlord,' cried Palmer, 'have you no horses at all?'

'No, sir, I'm very sorry, but no — I have few customers,' replied that worthy, having stepped out of the corner into which he had retreated upon the entrance of the four men.

'Then I must borrow one of our friend's here,' commented Palmer.

'Why, but that's thieving!' cried the hairy man.

'No doubt it's strange to you,' snapped Palmer sarcastically. Then he called back over his shoulder: 'Have you them covered, Will?'

'Yes, Dick, that I have.'

'Then I'm off. Where are these villains taking my wife?' he asked the fat man.

'To the Monastery Inn,' replied Pedro, a sardonic grin on his greasy face.

'I'll see you there, Will, tonight.'

'Right, Dick,' replied Will, knowing what folly it was to question his young friend's decisions when he was in this kind of mood.

Dick Palmer turned and hastened from the room. Reaching one of the impostor's horses, he mounted and galloped off at a great pace down the path to the high road. As he entered the main road and turned left he realised he had not asked the landlord where the nearest bridge over the river was situated. It could not be helped; he would have to ride until he came to one.

His thoughts were wild and mixed as he rode, but he knew that the main thing was to reach Red Ruby still tied to the big rock on the plain. It seemed it was a long time since he left her, but in actual fact not eight hours had passed by.

On Palmer raced, digging in his spurs and fretting at the slow pace of the grey mare he had stolen. The sooner he was in the saddle on Red Ruby the better, for there the former highwayman was at home. All the time he kept a sharp lookout for a bridge but time passed and still he had not reached one.

Abruptly Palmer reined in and contemplated the fast flowing river close by the road. He gritted his teeth, pressed his black tricorn hat firmly down on his head and swung the horse down the bank and through the high grass and thick bushes that grew there in profusion. With his heart in his mouth Palmer guided the horse straight down and the animal, realising his intention, bravely leaped forward into the river and in a moment the rider felt the waters swirling about his thighs.

Grimly Dick held on tight and firmly coaxed his steed towards the opposite bank. In the middle of the river the current was very powerful and Palmer felt the horse struggling with all its strength to withstand the insidious drag of the water. Cursing to himself he realised that now they were making little headway and were on the verge of being swept sideways. The water frothed about them gleefully, as if enjoying the battle.

'Come on,' cried Dick anxiously, 'come on me girl,' and he slapped the horse's damp buttocks. 'One final effort.'

The grey mare, her head only a few inches out of the water, spluttered and coughed, then she appeared to take new heart for all at once they were forging ahead again. Palmer gasped with relief for the worst of the crossing was over. In a moment he felt the horse touch the bed of the river and then she had scrambled out and gamely clambered up the steep bank.

Palmer patted her neck and then spurred forward again in the direction of the rocky plain. About them now were thick, dark forests broken here and there by lush meadows, not at all like the plain where stood the Pack Horse Inn. Dick began to wonder whether he was travelling in the right direction, but, as he topped a rise he saw some distance ahead, nestling in its little valley, the tavern by the name of 'Travellers' Hollow'.

Thereupon he turned south and in a few moments, galloping up a steep, grassy bank, he beheld the plateau and with a glad heart espied the big rock with two horses standing patiently beneath it. Dick was still some distance away when one of the horses turned round and at sight of the rider, began a shrill whinny in a highly excited manner. At this the second horse also began whinnying and by the time Palmer had reached the rock Red Ruby and Will's black stallion were straining at their reins and generally acting in a most exuberant fashion.

Dick Palmer grinned, dismounted, and hurried over to Red Ruby and clasped her noble head in his arms, and the highly strung mare muzzled her nose beneath Palmer's long coat and snuffled about with great pleasure at the return of her master. Will Snell's black stallion, having glanced about and realised that his master had not returned, now stood still, her head lowered dejectedly.

Palmer patted his massive flanks reassuringly, then he mounted Red Ruby and led the other two horses towards the Pack Horse Inn. Jeremy Mathering's and Jonathan Stark's steeds were still there, standing dolefully in the shadow of the inn. Palmer led the whole troup back along the road to the Travellers' Hollow.

There he spoke to the girl, who was delighted to see him again, and asked her to quarter the four horses until their owners collected them. Palmer conjectured that when his friends returned and found their horses missing they would enquire at once at this inn.

'Please give the chestnut mare food and drink and a brush down, for I must ride to London this very moment.'

'This moment?' cried the pretty girl aghast, 'but surely you can stay for a tankard of ale?'

'Yes, I can, whilst the horse is prepared for the road.'

The young girl handed Red Ruby over to an ancient rustic, who was presumably the ostler, and he meandered off behind the inn with the high-stepping chestnut mare.

As Dick Palmer sat and quaffed his ale the girl chatted away to him about this and that, but the gist of her conversation failed to penetrate his mind, for he was thinking of his wife, Jeanette. Deep within him there was a great fear, the like of which he had not experienced since his adventure in Epping Forest when he had met Jeanette Murray, or Penfield as was her real name.

Meditating thus on the past he remembered the villainous Adam Penfield, Squire of High Beach, who was Jeanette's father, and his equally villainous second wife, Charlotte. It was Penfield who had schemed to obtain his first wife's — Jeanette's mother's — fortune, and in doing he had tried to kill Jeanette, to whom the fortune rightfully belonged. Penfield's scheme had failed and he had died as a result, but Charlotte had escaped and Palmer often wondered whether the evil woman had ever been caught. It was during this adventure that he had first met the great Will Snell; but now his thoughts were interrupted by the return of the ancient ostler leading Red Ruby. The beautiful animal was shining with good health, and generally she appeared in fine fettle.

'Ha,' cried Dick, finishing his ale and tending the girl a silver coin. 'Many thanks ostler, do you think she's ready for a long ride?'

'Why certainly sire,' croaked the ostler, 'she's as fit as meself!'

Thinking this a somewhat doubtful recommendation but trusting the old man's word, Palmer mounted and with a wave, was off down the road like a thunderbolt.

We shall not bore the reader with Dick Palmer's ride to London, for nothing directly concerning this tale occurred on the journey. It is sufficient to say that he raced through the countryside and through the villages and towns at truly a great speed and the local rustics stood back, open-mouthed, and marvelled that man could travel so fast. It was a little after midday that he saw ahead the pretty, white façade of his home set serenely amongst the neat lawns and flower beds.

Now the pangs of anxiety struck at his heart as he grew nearer and he slowed to a mere trot, almost fearing to enter the drive. However, realising he was wasting time, he galloped grim-faced through the gateway and swept up to the front of the house, glancing here and there for sign of Jeanette.

12

Dick Palmer leaped from his horse and stood staring about the house, realising with dismay that if there had been any occupants of his home they would have by now heard the sound of his horse and rushed to the door to see who the visitor might be.

There was an empty feeling in Palmer's stomach as he stepped into the house and began searching the rooms on the ground floor. Now and again, when he returned to the passage, he shouted out his wife's name and then that of Nicholas Wilken's, and he stood listening for a reply but there was none. The house was silent; everything was in its place and it seemed as if the occupants were only away temporarily, for in the kitchen a wood fire crackled merrily and the oven door at the side stood open.

Looking out the kitchen window on the stable yard at the back Palmer could see one of his horses in its stable placidly eating hay, as if nothing was amiss. But a stable adjoining was empty, the black mare missing. Quickly Dick ran out and across the yard and stared into the stable — it was quite empty and the saddle and harness were gone. Grimly Dick turned about and surveyed his home — a hopeless terror engulfed him and he felt like crying. But instead he patted his capacious pockets of his long coat wherein resided his two trusty pistols and re-crossed the yard to the house, intending to search the upper rooms.

When he had accomplished this he realised he would have to sit down and consider very seriously his next move. He could not afford now to make any mistakes or blunders. To reach a decision, however, did not appear to be a very hard task — Pedro, the oily man, had intimated she was to be taken to the Monastery Inn — and it was there that Dick obviously had better go as soon as he was assured nothing could be gained by remaining at his home. What connection the Monastery Inn had with Toby-Joy he had yet to discover, but that there was a connection somewhere he was convinced. Then where in the scheme of things came 'The Lady' to whom all referred, but of whom few appeared to know anything about?

Dick Palmer felt instinctively that this woman was the mastermind behind the evil workings of Toby-Joy and that her apprehension and unveiling would provide the solution to the whole affair, including the strange, deliberate impersonation of Will Snell and himself. But now time was against him, for was it not tonight that Pedro had said there was to be a meeting at Toby-Joy? And his beautiful wife, Jeanette, was missing.

The more Dick Palmer thought about the matter the greater became his anger; in fact, a seething rage mounted within him with every moment that passed. His fury, however, was well restrained yet, nevertheless, he could not conceal it completely and his youthful features reflected his feelings. He climbed the narrow staircase to the upper rooms of the house, and his face was a stony, colourless mask out of which his blue eyes stared with a strange intensity.

It was in this mood that Dick Palmer entered Jeanette's bedroom at the front of the house and there beheld Nicholas Wilken stretched out on the floor, an ugly gash on the side of his head.

Palmer rushed forward and dropped on to one knee at Naughty Nick's side. He felt the boy's pulse and with relief realised that he was only unconscious. Dick patted Nicholas' cheeks and tried to bring him round but it was of no avail. He jumped to his feet again and ran downstairs to the kitchen. There he found a glass and, filling it with water, hurried back to the bedroom.

He halted on the threshold, glass in hand, for there was Wilken sitting up and tenderly feeling the gash on his temple. The boy's big brown eyes lighted up at the sight of his master and he smiled with joyful relief.

'Take this water, Nick,' said Palmer, and the boy thankfully accepted the glass and drank greedily from it. Dick helped him into a chair and then waited patiently for Nicholas to speak and explain what had happened.

At last the boy's eyes regained a little of their customary sparkle and, whilst Palmer tended his wound, he told of what had befallen at the house.

'It was not an hour ago, sir, they were two big fellows that comes suddenly riding up the drive as bold as you wish. I was in the yard sweeping and I stopped and stares, for these two coves walks straight into the house as if they owns it.'

Nicholas Wilken's elfin face abruptly screwed up with pain as Palmer pulled the bandage too tight. 'Sorry Nick — carry on.'

'Well, naturally, I drops me broom and takes meself quickly to the front and there I sees these two rough looking intruders standing in the passage and staring about them with some uncertainty.

' 'Where's your mistress, lad?' asks one.

' 'Upstairs,' says I. 'May I venture to ask what you require'?'

' 'Never you mind,' replies the first man, and then both of them takes themselves up the stairs and disappears.

'I runs up after 'em and as I reaches the top I hears a scream and I rushes into the mistress's bedroom to behold them struggling furiously with her.

'I hastens forward an' as I do I hears one of the rogues say: 'Take it easy, Pete, you know what the Lady said — not to 'urt 'er 'till we got 'er to the inn.'

'The other fellow sees me coming and drawing a pistol he swings it at me, an' then everything went as black as night. That's it, sir. The next thing I remembers is you coming through the door there.'

'Thank you, Nick,' whispered Dick Palmer, and there was a cold glare in his eyes as he slowly stepped back and sat down heavily on the bed. 'Not to hurt her till we get her to the inn,' he repeated in a low voice. 'So — there is a chance yet.'

'What are you going to do, Master Dick?'

'Why,' cried Palmer, jumping to his feet again, 'go after 'em, of course. You say this was but an hour ago?'

'Yes.'

'Then I must fly, Nick. I think I know the inn they mentioned.'

'God be with you, Master Dick,' exclaimed Nicholas fervently.

'Will you be all right now then, Nick?'

'Why certainly, sir, but I wish I was coming with you.'

'Ha, when you are a little older, Nick; then I shall be proud to ride at your side. Farewell!' and Palmer turned and strode swiftly from the room.

Nicholas Wilken moved to the window and watched his master mount, and it struck him that never before had he seen Dick Palmer with such a white, terrible look upon his face. Wilken remained at the window till his master was out of sight and then he collapsed on the bed, thinking about the abduction of his mistress and feeling greatly reassured now that Dick Palmer was on the trail.

13

At the 'Jocular Jack' Will Snell, pistol in hand, advanced upon the three men at the bar. 'Now then gentlemen,' cried he, 'you have a number of things to tell my friends and me.'

With an oath, Pedro, the oily man, drew a wicked looking knife and with surprising swiftness leaped at Will Snell. The giant was caught unawares, for had never thought the man would try such a wild effort to escape. It would have gone ill with Will if Pedro had reached him — his pistol was not even cocked. But there was rescue at hand, for the sound of a shot echoed and re-echoed around the taproom.

Pedro appeared to halt in mid-air, gave a choking and fell dead at Will's feet with a solid thump. The giant gazed in some consternation at the body of the oily man not through dismay at the fellow's sudden death, but through realising that he had been very near his own death. Will slowly turned round and saw Jonathan Stark feet apart, grimly holding a smoking pistol in his hand.

'Bountiful thanks, Jonathan — the rascal would have driven his knife into me before I could have taken a breath.'

The dangerous glint that was in Stark's dark eyes quickly faded and he smiled slightly. 'That I could see, Will.'

Jeremy Mathering stepped up to the remaining two men and, waving his pistol at them, cried: 'Now, rogues, tell us about Toby-Joy.'

'Hold hard, Jeremy,' cried Will, 'I think it would be a better proposition to take 'em out in yonder wood, and then I am sure they will tell us all we want to know.'

Jeremy nodded. 'A fine idea, Will.' From his great height he glared down upon the prisoners and they, realising what was afoot, looked thoroughly frightened.

'Why,' cried Will, 'but you're poor representatives of Dick Palmer and myself. Come on, out you go.' The two imposters' weapons were taken from them and then they were unceremoniously bundled out of the

Jocular Jock and ushered deep into the wood that surrounded the inn.

Coming to a tiny glade, where thick bushes screened them from prying eyes, they halted and the two men were pushed to the ground and stood over by Will Snell and Jeremy Mathering.

'Now,' said Jeremy, his lean frame towering above and seeming like one of the many saplings that abounded in the wood. 'Toby-Joy — what is it?'

The shifty youth, his pale eyes full of fear, cried out: 'Nay, but we don't know.'

'Ha,' roared Will, 'yet you were going there — one moment me excellent coves,' and the giant stepped to the edge of the glade, broke off a thin, whippy branch and then returned, a wicked gleam in his blue eyes. He raised it high above his head, and indeed, with the slanting rays of the sun glinting upon his red hair, he appeared a most atrocious looking fellow, so that there was good reason for the shifty youth's scream of fright.

'I'll tell you,' he cried, 'we don't know. Pedro was taking us there.'

'He speaks the truth,' growled the hairy man. 'We've never bin there before.'

Will lowered the whip and snapped: 'Who told you to use my name then, and that of Dick Palmer?'

'It was the Lady,' said the black-haired fellow. 'We met 'er at the Monastery Inn, an' she paid us ten pounds each to ride the country and broadcast that we were you and Palmer.'

'And this woman,' interposed Jonathan Stark, staring keenly down at the hairy man, 'you have never met her before?'

'No — she suggested the idea one night we were staying there.'

'Where did you meet Pedro?'

'At Littlehampton, 'e said the Lady — as she is known — 'ad invited us to a place called Toby-Joy where there would be plenty of song and ale.'

'You don't know why the woman wanted you to impersonate Will Snell and Dick Palmer?'

'No — we were not particularly interested either.'

'One more question,' said Stark quietly,

then rapped out: 'Do you know Simon Pendexter?'

There was a guilty flash in the hairy fellow's eyes as he glanced about the glade, avoiding the hypnotic look of Jonathan Stark.

'Tell me,' rasped the sharp-featured man, and the note in his deep voice bode ill for the hairy man if he failed to reply.

'Yes,' grunted the fellow after a pause, 'we 'ave worked for 'im many a time. Pedro is one of 'is men — that is 'e was.'

'And you don't know what Toby-Joy is?'

Jeremy Mathering began pacing up and down the glade like a tiger. Will Snell shrugged his great shoulders: 'It's useless,' he grunted, turning away from the two men on the ground, 'they know nothing of value.'

'I avow it seems so,' commented Jonathan. 'It was unfortunate that this rogue Pedro had to die — he might have told us something.'

'Ha — let's get off,' cried Jeremy, we're wasting our time.'

'What about these fine rascals?' asked Stark.

'Let's take 'em to the nearest constable,' suggested Will, swishing his stick through the air, 'then we had better collect our steeds on that rocky plain and make for the Monastery Inn. It seems that the gang are meeting at Toby-Joy tonight and our first stepping-stone should be the Monastery Inn — Dick said he would meet us there. This time we must search the place with a fine tooth comb.'

'It's a good plan,' agreed Jonathan Stark, 'I'll go and ask the landlord where the nearest constable abides,' and he strode off swiftly through the trees towards the inn.

Will Snell watched the lithe, broad-shouldered frame of Stark as it passed through the wood, noting the swashbuckling sailor-like gait of the man, and Will felt sure that Stark was no stranger to a ship on the high seas. Musing in this manner the giant was rudely awakened by a cry from Jeremy Mathering.

'Will — behind you!'

Will twisted about and caught sight of 'Shifty' leaping at him — with the neighbourly intention of burying a tiny knife in his back. Will did not relish the idea at all and, as he swung round, he swung out his great arm and caught the youth in mid-air and sent the fellow crashing to the ground.

Will waggled one large finger at his attacker, who crawled back beside 'Hairy' in a most crestfallen fashion and cried: 'Now, me young fella, that was a most unkind and foolish thing to do — I have a good mind to beat the daylights out of that skinny frame of yours.'

The youth scowled and made no reply, and then footsteps were heard coming through the forest and Jonathan Stark stepped into the glade again.

'There's a constable at a village by the name of Pulborough not two miles up the road,' he announced.

'Good,' cried Jeremy, 'let's shepherd these rogues to the inn, use their steeds and be on our way.'

The two prisoners were jerked to their feet and the five men returned to the inn. Finding a short piece of rope, Will tied Hairy's right hand to Shifty's left, and then he mounted one of the horses whilst Jonathan and Jeremy mounted the other.

'Off you trot,' roared Will at the two men on the ground, and they, looking most dejected, stumbled off up the path to the high road, with the three mounted men leisurely bringing up the rear. They were followed by a roar of laughter from the bald-headed landlord, and cursing, muttering and spitting, the prisoners shambled along with great ignominy. In a little while, when only a few paces up the road, the prisoners began cursing one another, for their difference in size and physique made it awkward for them to run smoothly together. They jostled and bumped against each other and naturally Shifty had the worst of the exchange, and such was his language that Will Snell, with a pained expression clapped his hands over his ears.

And so they entered the tiny village of Pulborough.

At once a small crowd of laughing and gaping locals gathered about the party, and the more cheeky of them touched and prodded the prisoners with great glee and curiosity.

'Avast, brethren,' roared Will, 'where's the constable?'

Several people pointed down the road and one jovial red-faced fellow cried: 'At the last cottage on the right mister. Who are your prisoners?'

'They are two of the gang who have been taking your womenfolk,' replied Will.

At this the crowd gave a roar and swiftly they changed from a throng of joking villagers to an ugly mob, and Hairy and Shifty blanched with fear and the latter gazed appealingly up at his captors. Two or three villagers brutally kicked the prisoners and the hostile excitement swiftly mounted.

Seeing the danger, Jonathan Stark and Jeremy Mathering rode up quickly along one side of the two men and Will rode up on the other side. Thus they moved slowly up the village street, with the crowd following, shouting and gesticulating, but the three men managed to keep them at bay; and so they arrived at the constable's cottage.

This worthy was an extremely large man with grey, bushy side-whiskers, red face and a paunch indicative of good living. He stood at the gate in his shirtsleeves and puffed out his cheeks and frowned impressively.

'Hey — hey, and vot's this?'

Will Snell dismounted. 'Greetings, officer,' said he, and the constable blew out his cherubic cheeks the more. 'I bring into your safe and wise custody two prisoners who are members of the gang that marauds hereabouts.'

'Hey — hey,' grunted the constable, and with some pomp opened his gate and waved Will and his prisoners inside. 'Bring the pigs within, my man, away from these babbling idiots.'

The 'idiots' appeared to like this, for they gave a cheer, and Will, pushing the two before him, followed the constable into the neat little cottage.

'Now tell the officer,' cried Will to Hairy and Shifty, 'what imposters you are.'

Hairy scratched his great growth of black hair and hesitated: 'Tell 'im what

— that we 'ave been using your name?'

'Yes — and my friend, Dick Palmer's.'

'We were given orders,' growled Hairy, 'to pretend we were Will Snell and Dick Palmer.'

'Hey, hey,' cried the constable, puffing, 'an' vot for?'

'I don't know.'

The constable looked somewhat vacant, but he was equal to the occasion. 'Right, my man, I will lock 'em up. Their story can be told later.'

'Then I and Dick Palmer are released from all blame for their roguish activities?'

'Who are you?' asked the constable.

'Will Snell.'

'Ha, I see. Vell, if these fellows say they have been masquerading as you, then I s'pose it does.'

'Thank you, constable. Will you tell the law officers that are in the neighbourhood we are not guilty?'

'Hey, hey,' puffed the constable, 'now I remember. They have a warrant for you, haven't they? Yes, they passed through the village only yesterday, and I am expecting them back.'

Will breathed heavily. 'Good, then you'll tell them?'

'I vill, me man — these two rascals were impersinnatin' you, eh?'

'C'rect,' replied Will, 'and tell the officers this — we now seek the gang of villains at the Monastery Inn. That's their headquarters, so we reckon.'

'Hey, hey,' cried the constable, leading off his prisoners with great pride. 'I will tell 'em, ne'er you worry.'

Will Snell rejoined his companions outside the cottage. He turned to one of the villagers: 'Which is the way, friend, to the Pack Horse Inn?'

The villager pointed along the road. 'Up the street, mister, an' over the bridge yonder an' you cannot fail to see it, it's near the inn called 'Travellers' Hollow'.'

'Many thanks, pal,' replied Will, mounting his horse. In a moment, with Jonathan and Jeremy on the second steed, they were galloping away up the village street.

Jeremy sat behind Jonathan and gazed ahead with an intent expression on his long face, his thoughts being of his sister, Crimson, and how she was faring. Stark's thoughts, as always now, were of Simon Pendexter and of the revenge he sought. Will Snell rode at the side of his companion in a meditative frame of mind. He and Dick Palmer had succeeded in proving their innocence of the crimes committed by Hairy and Shifty and thus had upheld their reputations and honour. But why had it all started in the first place? That was what they must find out.

Will's thoughts centred on Crimson Mathering and a strange light entered his eyes, a light that can only be described as dreamy. He grew worried when he remembered she was now a captive of Simon Pendexter, and he felt his bandages tenderly; with these thoughts he abruptly spurred his steed to a faster pace.

In a short while they came upon a break in the trees on their right and the three men espied an arched, stone bridge spanning the river, which sparkled in the bright sunlight. They passed over the bridge without slowing their pace and now the rough lane wound through a deep forest, where the light was dim and the atmosphere oppressive. Overhead, on top of the foliage and in the sunlight, the birds chirrupped and chattered in a great chorus of song, but beneath there was deep silence. As they rode the three men found it hard to believe that amongst these lovely surroundings, amongst these joyful sounds, there was such a man as Simon Pendexter.

Now the forest was behind and they traversed pleasant hill and dale and all about them were many shades of green — the green of the hedgerows, of the fields and of the trees. All at once they cantered down a gentle slope to a crossroads.

'Ha,' cried Will, 'these are the roads we passed over when riding to the Inn by the River. Travellers' Hollow can't be a stone's throw away.'

'You're right, Will,' said Jonathan, glancing keenly about, 'and I mind that it's midday.'

'Yes,' said Jeremy, 'and I mind that me throat is parched and my belly empty.'

'It's the Travellers' Hollow for us, then,'

announced Will, and he swung his horse into the road leading south. Within a few moments they came upon the inn, looking as neat and as placid as ever.

At once the pretty girl, Agnes, came running out from the cool darkness of the taproom, smiling delightedly. 'Why, it's the three hungry gentlemen — the other gentleman said you would come,' she cried, dancing around her guests. 'Your steeds are quartered in our stable.'

'Ha, then Palmer brought them here?' asked Stark, seating himself at a table.

'Yes — he was in a mighty hurry and was gone like the shot from a cannon.'

'I can well believe it,' grunted Will, joining Jonathan at the table. 'Now, Agnes, what about it?'

'Ha, sir, and you want a meal I presume and no doubt a pint of ale?'

'But of course.'

'Then Master Will, you cannot eat yet.'

'Cannot eat?' cried the giant, frowning, 'and how's that — have you no food?'

'Oh, but yes, some very tasty morsels, but you, Master Will, shall have that awful bandage removed first and your wound bathed.'

Jonathan Stark and Jeremy Mathering burst into roars of laughter, and Will turned and glared at them in a most fearsome manner.

'And what's the matter with you?' asked he.

'Think of me, Will,' grinned Jonathan, 'whilst you are being nursed. I shall be quaffing cool, sparkling tankards of ale and eating succulent pieces of beef roasted!'

'Come, Master Will,' cried Agnes, shaking her dark curls, 'you must be tended to at once. I promise I shall not take long.'

Will Snell gave a heavy groan and rose wearily to his feet and Agnes took his great hand in her tiny one and led him into the inn. Whilst they were gone the ancient ostler appeared carrying a tray loaded with cold beef roasted and chicken and salad and two pints of ale. These were placed before Stark and Mathering and the two men settled down in silence to the task of slaking their thirsts and quenching their appetites.

14

Some time after, when Jonathan and Jeremy had taken their fill and the latter was puffing happily at his briar, Agnes came trotting out with a tray of food and drink and behind her came Will Snell with a new bandage and looking greatly refreshed, and eyeing ravenously the food carried by his hostess.

Without a word Will sat down by his friends and ate and drank with great energy, making quite a to do about the matter, and his antics highly amused Agnes who was standing close by watching him. At last he had finished and he sat back and beamed round at his audience.

'Well, Agnes,' he said, 'that's mighty nice — now will you have our steeds saddled?'

'Why certainly Master Will, at once,' she replied. 'It's unfortunate that you must leave so early.'

'I agree, it is — but it's most necessary I assure you. Thanks again for tending to this large head o' mine.'

'What time is it Agnes?' asked Stark.

'I'll see for you,' she answered, and off she tripped into the inn. She popped her pretty head out again: 'It's five past three o'clock sir — I go now to see to your horses,' and she disappeared.

'Which is it to be?' asked Will Snell, 'the Inn by the River or the Monastery Inn?'

'The Monastery Inn,' replied Jeremy. 'It's there that my sister, Crimson, was taken, and there that Dick said he would meet us.'

'I agree,' exclaimed Will, stroking his new bandage. 'There lies the solution I think, to Toby-Joy as well.'

Jonathan Stark said: 'Yes, that should be our objective, for we have our steeds and I'm certain it's the Monastery Inn that Pendexter is aiming for upon his return.'

'Perhaps we shall meet this lady, whoever she might be,' said Will. 'She ordered those two coves to impersonate

Dick and myself.'

'Yes, and the same woman invited them to Toby-Joy,' asked Jeremy.

Will Snell rose as their horses were brought to the front by the ancient ostler. 'Yes, my good friends, I think I shall enjoy meeting this lady, for she seems to be the root of all our troubles.' Then he added, half to himself: 'Very strange. I wonder who she can be? It seems she seeks the destruction of Dick and I.'

'Ha, but she's not the root of my trouble,' muttered Jonathan Stark as he walked towards his steed.

Will Snell turned to Jeremy and whispered: 'Nay, Jeremy, I don't fancy Pendexter's luck with our resourceful friend after 'im.'

They joined Stark, mounted their horses and were made ready for the road. Will's black stallion was making a great to do about having his master seated upon him again, and the magnificent animal was pawing the ground and quivering with excitement and his desire to be speeding along the highway once more.

'My, it's not the same to ride a strange

steed,' grunted the giant, patting his horse's neck affectionately. 'Are we ready?'

Jonathan and Jeremy indicated that they were, and then Will turned to Agnes, who stood on the threshold of the inn. 'Avast, Agnes — farewell. I shall mind your hospitality this many a day, and shall make a point to return.'

The girl waved and cried out: 'Farewell,' and the three men dug spur into horse's flank and were away, galloping back along the road to the Monastery Inn.

Perhaps they might have hesitated, or at least given some thought to the matter, had they but known what the future held in store for them.

They rode swiftly north, keen to reach the Monastery Inn again and discover the secret of Toby-Joy. They passed over the crossroads and continued on across the sparsely wooded rolling countryside. In a little while they entered a deep forest and must needs slow down for the rough road wound and twisted through in a haphazard manner. As they swept round one sharp bend they came upon a fallen tree that lay across the way, and they now had to slow to a trot to thread their way through its leafy branches.

Suddenly there was a great swishing noise and many cries and shouts and from the foliage above three men dropped like stones on to each of the riders' backs.

'Avast,' roared Will, 'We are ambushed!'

The three men vainly tried to save themselves from being hurled from their steeds, but the weight of their attackers was too much and they fell, locked in combat, to the ground.

Directly they had become dislodged, the trees on either side of the highway seemed to come alive and from all points divers evil-looking men threw themselves into the fray.

There was no time for further speech now and Will Snell found himself fighting three men at once. Jonathan Stark had produced a knife and was lashing out most effectively, but he was beset by four silent brutes who, equipped with clubs, replied with equal energy. Out of the corner of his eye Will saw Jeremy, on his feet, towering over four unshaven rogues who, bit by bit, were dragging him down to the dusty road.

Jonathan Stark suddenly fell forward on his face, but as he fell to the ground he looked ahead and the last Will heard of him was a string of seafaring curses, for Stark had espied a blonde giant standing in the middle of the road, a grin upon his lips, nonchalantly twirling a spiked ball at the end of a leather thong.

Jeremy Mathering found himself pinned to the ground, unable to make a move and, seeing this, Will Snell fought with even greater fury. He could not see the wood for it seemed he was fighting scores of men at one and the same time. He was still on his feet, swinging his great arms like a windmill, then, without warning, he felt a crushing blow on the back of his head and suddenly found his legs crumble beneath him and he collapsed into oblivion.

When Will awoke it was to find that he and his companions were being dragged along the highway by ropes attached to their horses. The giant felt a terrible aching and stinging pain about his arms and legs and he hastily scrambled to his feet; and almost at the same time Jonathan Stark did likewise. Jeremy Mathering had apparently recovered consciousness earlier, for he was trotting along behind Will's black stallion, his doleful face a mixture of rage and apprehension. Will glanced down at the back of his hands, tied together by the rope, and saw that they were grievously scratched and torn.

He realised they had been dragged along the road whilst they were unconscious. He shuddered at the thought of what might have happened to them had they not recovered consciousness so quickly, and Will Snell thanked his lucky stars. He did not fancy the idea of waking up to find one's arms and kneecaps completely worn away.

Three men rode their horses, one of them being Simon Pendexter and it was behind his steed that Jonathan Stark ran. So they traversed the highway, a man running on ahead to ensure they met no stranger without due warning, and nearly half a score more wild-eyed brutes ambled along with the captives. The horses were travelling at a fast trot and the three prisoners soon discovered it required all their attention to keep with them; once they slowed down then over they would topple on to the hard, dusty road — and be dragged to their death.

The whole party moved in silence and at first Will wondered at this — the rough looking crew should surely want to tease them in their predicament — but he realised that the gang did not wish to attract attention, for it was still daylight, and the peace officers might be in the neighbourhood.

'I avow,' called Jonathan to Will, 'We're in a fine pickle — what do you think?'

Will nodded grimly, but gave no answer for he was heavier than Stark and needed every ounce of breath he could gain. Will Snell, for once in his life, felt a certain wavering of spirit, for he was now beginning to realise with what kind of a man they were faced. The giant stared at the jogging back of Pendexter and a feeling of sickening horror engulfed him at the thought that such an evil, ruthless, cruel man could exist. Man? — he was no man, he was a brute, a wild beast, with all the feelings and senses of a wild beast.

Will's gasps came now quick and fast, for they had travelled nearly a mile. Glancing sideways at Jonathan and Jeremy he saw that they were in the same state and there were desperate expressions on their faces. Will glanced anxiously forward hoping to see the Monastery Inn, but he recognised that part of the highway along which they were now travelling and knew that the inn still lay a number of furlongs ahead.

Gritting his teeth he stumbled wearily along behind the horse, its hind quarters seeming to sway back and forth mockingly. Never before had Will realised how infuriating could be the rear view of a quadruped.

The procession continued on its grim way, now out on the open road, but hemmed in by high, thick hedgerows. Any workers in the fields would but see three horsemen and thus pay scant attention. If they met anyone on the road, then Will was sure the unfortunate person would never escape to tell what he or she had seen. The giant found that he had to watch his footsteps carefully, for a trip on the uneven surface of the road might mean a fall, and he knew that if he fell now he might never regain his feet.

To add to their discomfort the horses' hooves kicked up a gritty dust cloud behind them and, panting as the prisoners were, the dust irritated their throats and stung their eyes. This reached such a pitch that soon the three men were coughing, spitting and crying, vainly trying to reach up to their eyes with their bound hands. When but an inch or so away, the horses would suddenly step a little faster and the prisoners' hands would be drawn away again.

Still the motley crowd around them made no remark, but just padded along at their side, for all the world like a pack of dumb animals. Simon Pendexter paid no attention whatsoever to the state of his prisoners, but sat his horse like an evil idol, cold and distant and so the torture continued. But at last there was a slowing down and raising his cut face Will's bloodshot eyes saw ahead the Monastery Inn and he heaved a great sigh of relief. But his relief was short-lived for he quickly realised that no doubt worse was in store for them, and all at once icy fingers of despair clutched at the giant's heart.

The grey inn lay silent, brooding beneath the tall trees that half-encircled it. Simon Pendexter dismounted and walked back with a smile on his red, well-proportioned features, but his pale, watery eyes held a light of devilish anticipation. The ropes were detached from the horses and Pendexter led his three prisoners like dogs into the cool darkness of the inn, and the rest of the gang trooped in after him.

15

Dick Palmer had not ridden far from London on the road to the Monastery Inn when he realised that he would have to stop for a short time to give his chestnut mare, Red Ruby, a rest. He had deliberately not changed to the old stallion left in the stable at his home, as he was slow and tired quickly. But he might need a fresh horse later on, and so he looked out for a wayside inn where Red Ruby could be given a drink and a rub down.

Palmer was on edge and deep down inside there was a strange empty feeling. But also there was a terrible rage that seethed within him, and his mood was shown in his pale, tense face and staring eyes. As he rode he could tell that Red Ruby was exceedingly weary by the sweat on her flanks and the way she nodded her head up and down with each step, as if forcing herself to keep up the pace demanded of her. Dick knew his fine steed would never slow down until she was told and would go on until she dropped from sheer exhaustion.

Soon he entered a large village and immediately espied a great inn by the name of 'The Black Bear', and he rode into the spacious courtyard and dismounted. At once an ostler appeared.

'Arternoon, sir,' said he.

'I require food and drink and a rub down for my steed: we're in a hurry.'

'Right, sir, an' a fine courser she is. I'll attend to 'er meself, sir.'

The ostler led Red Ruby away and Dick Palmer walked over to a corner of the yard where there were a number of tables and chairs. He ordered a pint of ale and, when it arrived, drank thirstily. Then he sat back and stared gloomily at the cobbled stones of the yard.

'Cheer up, pal, it might never 'appen!'

Glancing sideways Palmer saw a fat jovial-looking person sprawled at the neighbouring table. He was dressed in a most brilliant fashion with bright blue coat edged with gold braid and a magnificent multi-coloured flowered waist-coat that was stretched tight over his great paunch.

'Hope it doesn't — God willing,' grunted Dick in reply

'An' what's the trouble, pal? You can tell Augustus Figgins, of 'Figgins, Figgins and Snott, solicitors'.'

'It's a private matter,' replied Palmer.

'Ha, but that's my living,' cried Mr. Figgins, 'private matters.'

'You can do no good, thank you; it's a matter for action, not talk.'

'Then it's a certainty you need a solicitor. Ne'er take action without the 'go ahead' from such as me.'

'I need no go ahead, thanks.'

'Dear, dear, so you 'ave already gone ahead — and without a lawyer.' Mr. Figgins shook his head sadly: 'Dear, dear — nay, young man, I can see you're 'eading for jail!'

To this cheerful prophecy Dick Palmer made no reply but quaffed his ale with some impatience.

'You're wanting to get on your way, I see,' continued Mr. Figgins persistently.

'Mind, take my advice — and it's worth a lot — don't make a move without a lawyer.'

Still Dick Palmer did not answer but rapped the table with the tips of his fingers and glared about the yard.

'Ha, an' you're annoyed — worse still. Maybe,' said Mr. Higgins cheerfully, 'this private matter of yours is a case for the 'igh court. If so, then you can't defend yourself without such as me; an' if you don't defend yourself, why, I can see you swinging on the gallows!'

'Thanks very much.'

'Don't mention,' said Mr. Figgins, sipping his sherry, 'but I must admit I don't fancy seeing such a fine young man as yourself creaking on the gibbet.'

'Yes, it would be an unpleasant sight.'

At this moment the ostler reappeared leading Red Ruby, and the mare without a doubt now looked clean and fresh and stepped in a lively fashion over the cobblestones. Dick Palmer, with some relief, jumped to his feet and walked to meet them. He tipped the ostler liberally and mounted the mare.

'Mind, don't forget young man,' called Mr. Figgins. 'My h'advice is most valuable.'

'And most expensive I expect,' replied Dick, and with this parting shot he touched Red Ruby's flanks and trotted out of the inn courtyard. In a moment they were galloping on their way again and by the very feel of her Dick knew that Red Ruby was well refreshed.

They kept up a good pace, thundering over hill and dale, through quiet villages and silent forests, until some distance ahead Dick could see the cottages of Ewhurst. He passed the gates of Mathering Manor and wondered what the Squire was doing with all his family away; then Dick had left the village and was on the last lap to the Monastery Inn.

With a beating heart Palmer reached the top of the slope leading down to the inn and what he saw there made him swing Red Ruby swiftly into the shelter of the trees at the side of the highway. He leaped from his horse and, creeping forward to a point where he could watch the inn unseen, he observed, with dismay,

Simon Pendexter leading in Will Snell, Jonathan Stark and Jeremy Mathering at the end of ropes. Even from this distance he could see the weak, broken state of his friends, for they appeared to half-crawl into the inn. A cold despair gripped Dick and he sat down heavily on a rotting tree-trunk to think over the situation.

From his position Palmer could see the ruined monastery and, remembering the old gentleman's words, he contemplated the broken walls with renewed interest. Could it be that the answer to Toby-Joy lay amongst those ruins? He and Jeremy had drawn a blank in their search, but the old gentleman had been killed for what he had divulged. The young man gazed across to the monastery, its walls stark and jagged against the sky, and now they seemed to have a strange attraction and he suddenly resolved to visit the place again — now — and search for a clue with redoubled energy.

He rose and felt for his weapons and inspected them to see if they were loaded correctly, and then he realised that if he found his friends again, two pistols would prove of little use in assisting their escape.

With these thoughts Dick Palmer listened to the sound of a single horseman approaching along the highway with particular interest. Here was a way of supplementing his artillery. The traveller drew nearer and Dick ran back to his steed and mounted and waited in the cover of the trees.

The newcomer was deep in thought as he trotted leisurely along the road and thus was given a great surprise by Palmer as the latter spurred forward, pistol levelled, and accosted him.

'Hold hard, pal,' cried Dick.

'Oooh,' cried the traveller, an elderly, benign-looking fellow. 'Dear me! I have no valuables, rogue.'

'I don't require them. Throw me your weapons.'

The traveller stared in surprise but he was greatly relieved and immediately he plucked from his capacious pockets two long pistols and was about to throw them on the road when Palmer stopped him.

'Nay, pal, you'll buckle 'em; hand them to me.'

Without a word the traveller did as he was ordered and Dick placed the pistols in his own pockets. The traveller looked hopeful, hardly believing that he was to be let off so lightly.

'Have you no knives?'

'Knives?' cried the traveller aghast. 'Dear me, but I never carry such things.'

'Then off ye go.'

Not waiting for more the traveller dug in his spurs and galloped away down the hill towards the Monastery Inn, delighted that he had escaped the meeting with only the loss of his pistols.

Dick returned to the shelter of the wood and stared over the tops of the trees again at the ruined monastery. Its broken towers and walls seemed to be beckoning him; and all at once Palmer was convinced that there lay the solution to Toby-Joy. He looked down in the direction of the inn and was struck by the fact that no signs of life emanated from it, though nearly a score of men had entered but half an hour ago. Then Palmer began thinking of the woman he had seen at the window whose face seemed familiar, and he ruminated on the mystery for a few moments. Why had she arranged to have those two thieves impersonate Will and himself? Why? — to bring them to the Monastery Inn, of course. Yes, that was it. It certainly appeared that she required the capture of the two friends alive. Dick Palmer set out on foot for the ruined monastery with a certain notion in his brain that refused to be pushed aside.

He considered it would be safer to travel to the monastery on foot, for then he could escape attention and search amongst the ruins without molestation. Red Ruby was securely tied to a tree-trunk and he knew the mare would not move until he returned.

'That is,' murmured Dick to himself, 'if I do return.'

16

Palmer walked swiftly over the soft grass beneath the tall trees with a determined, grim air. His four pistols in his large coat pockets swung against his thighs as he strode along, and the feel and the sound of them gave a confident, devil-may-care air to the former highwayman, and when in this mood Dick Palmer was an exceedingly dangerous man.

The forest about him was quiet, for it was sunset and at this time the day-animals were preparing for slumber, and the night beasts had as yet not commenced their nocturnal wanderings. An odd bird here and there, high in the trees, suddenly chirruped or squawked and the call was answered from afar, then silence would fall again.

Palmer, however, was oblivious to his surroundings but he was alert for any strange sound, and one hand was never far from his pocket. Soon the ground began to slope upwards and Dick realised he was approaching the knoll upon which stood the ruined monastery. Now he moved with greater stealth, for if he was on the right track for Toby-Joy, then Simon Pendexter might have a few guards posted. In a moment he came out of the forest and above him lay the dark ruins of the monastery. Dick stood motionless for some time staring at the broken walls wondering if he would be able to discover the secret of Toby-Joy.

He was about to clamber up the grass slope and begin his search when there came a sound that froze the blood in his veins and he shrank back into the shelter of the trees. Borne to him on the gentle evening breeze was a wild, inane laugh:

'He, he, he!'

Dick's heart thumped against his ribs as he stared frantically about trying to make out from whence came the grim sound.

Again the terrible cackle rang out: 'He, he he!'

Dick's eyes gleamed for the laugh appeared to come from inside the monastery walls. He waited silently for the next laugh so that this time he could pinpoint its position. But time passed by and there was no repeat. Still Palmer waited and still the deathly hush that had settled over the ruins remained unbroken. Palmer at last took several stealthy steps forward and then stopped dead, for there now reached his ears a different sound — a shrill voice was raised in song!

Palmer retreated to the forest again and listened intently, and there was such a hysterical, ungovernable, high-pitched note about the voice that Palmer drew one of his pistols to reassure himself. He could hear quite clearly the words of the macabre song and they were as follows:-

Near this knoll lies Toby-Joy,
Near this knoll lies spiked boy,
Yo-ho-ho, an' plenty of drinkin'
Yo-ho-ho, and plenty of singin.'
Near at hand the ring is found,
The Lady too as king is crowned,
Yo-ho-ho, and plenty of drinkin',
Yo-ho-ho, and plenty of singin.'

The song ended and suddenly there came another 'he, he, he,' then a profound silence clothed the ruined monastery and the twilight accentuated the sinister atmosphere that pervaded the hilltop. Dropping to his knees, Dick Palmer began very slowly to crawl up the grass slope, keeping a keen watch meanwhile for any sight or sound of the weird human that hid amongst the ruins. But Palmer saw nothing and he reached the shadow of one of the broken walls with a queer feeling that he was not alone. He stood up, pistol in hand, expecting any moment to be attacked. But nothing happened and everything remained motionless, dark and quiet. Dick stepped quickly through an opening into the main hall of the monastery and he stood close by the wall where the iron ring was fitted to which he and Jeremy had tethered their horses on their previous visit. He stared about, gazing hard into the dark corners, and tried to discover the whereabouts of the strange singer. But the monastery seemed deserted.

Without warning there came the same high-pitched laugh, and this time it was directly behind Palmer. With a startled gasp he spun round, cocking his pistol at the same time and holding it out before him ready for immediate discharge.

Before him stood a weird-looking youth clad in long, flat shoes and a loose black coat that hung almost to his ankles. What with his staring eyes, pale face and unruly yellow hair waving in the breeze, he presented a wild, unnatural picture. Dick Palmer stared in amazement at the fellow for several moments. Then he snapped:

'Who are you?'

The youth smiled brightly and giggled and suddenly began waving his arms about, then he danced off across the monastery sward, his great coat swirling about him like a woman's skirt. Cheerfully he began singing again to himself.

'Who are you?' repeated Palmer, following him somewhat warily.

The wild youth stopped, turned and grinned at Palmer. 'Who am I?' he cried in a shrill voice. 'Why an' my name is William Tuggle.' Then abruptly his face changed and he added sadly: 'Though some do call me 'Wild Willie'.'

Dick Palmer lowered his pistol, for he now realised that Willie was quite harmless. 'Tell me, pal, that song of yours — you mention Toby-Joy. Where is this place?'

For reply the wild youth giggled again: 'He, he, he.' Then he was off dancing again, flitting about like a bat, with no sense or reason to his movements. So lightly did he move and so swiftly that he was suddenly standing behind Palmer again before the latter realised the fact. Dick spun round defensively but Willie just stood very upright and smiled, and it was then that Dick noticed a long scar, half hidden by his yellow hair, down the side of the youth's face.

They faced each other for several moments, one grim and uncertain, the other seemingly full of boisterous spirits.

'Now look, pal,' began Palmer again, 'I seek this place Toby-Joy. Where is it? You mention it in your song?'

'He, he, he,' replied Willie and went off dancing again, and as he pirouetted in the middle of the sward he chanted his strange song again:-

Near this knoll lies Toby-Joy,
Near this knoll lies spiked boy,
Yo-ho-ho, and plenty of drinkin',
Yo-ho-ho, and plenty of singin'.

'Where — where?' cried Palmer, running across to the youth and grasping him firmly by the arms. 'Come now, tell me, pal — it's a vital matter.'

Wild Willie released himself from Palmer's grip and stepped back and now there was a terrible glare upon his white face. 'It's in hell!' he screamed.

Dick cursed beneath his breath and realised that he could never force an answer from the wild youth He would have to plead with Willie. 'Look,' he said quietly, 'my wife and my friends are kidnapped and taken there, so it's natural that I seek the place.'

All at once Willie was smiling. 'He he he,' he chortled, and he was off again prancing about the ruined monastery.

Patiently Dick Palmer followed him,

waiting for his answer. Then the wild youth began singing the second verse:-

Near at hand the ring is found.

But he did not continue and instead began dancing around near the broken-down walls of the monastery. Suddenly Dick Palmer realised that Willie was trying to convey something to him in his own wild war. Dick followed him, watching his cavortings intently, and so they came to the opening through which Palmer had entered the monastery. Why had the youth only recited the first line of the second verse? What was it again? Ah, yes:-

Near at hand the ring is found.

What did it mean? Frantically Dick racked his brains for an answer. Wild Willie had stopped now by the opening and was grinning at Palmer as he approached. Then with a quick intake of breath Dick noticed that the youth was slowly describing a small circle with his right hand. He kept up the movement for some time, smiling away the while at Palmer. Then suddenly Dick Palmer recognised the motion. There could be no mistake. It was with such a twirling that Simon Pendexter swung his terrible spiked boy!

'So you know the villain,' grunted Dick grimly.

But the youth did not reply and all at once began pirouetting again before his companion, grinning and looking now and then out of the corner of his bright eyes at Dick Palmer. Then just behind Wild Willie Dick espied the iron ring affixed to the monastery wall. He glanced quickly at the youth but Willie seemed intent on his mad dance.

Could this ring and the one in the verse be the same, mused Palmer. He became excited and quickly stepped past Willie and placed his hand upon the rusty ring. Immediately the youth gave a great cackle of laughter and spun away across the sward, dancing about, it seemed, with even greater abandonment. It was his answer, Dick was sure, and he inspected the ring more closely. It was fixed to one of the large stones of which the wall consisted and was about three feet from the ground. Palmer wondered why it was there, what purpose did it or had it served? There appeared to be no reason for its presence in the wall.

Dick glanced over his shoulder to see what the wild youth was doing and he espied him standing motionless in the dusk watching, an expansive grin on his face. The moon had now risen and in its light Dick Palmer twisted the ring this way and that trying to discover its secret, but to no avail; nothing happened. Palmer persevered and he tried pulling the ring and now he obtained results.

Slowly the ring, as Dick pulled, came out of the wall on the end of an iron rod, and accompanying it there was a deep sound of grating and scraping like that of a drawbridge being raised. The ring came out a foot and then Palmer found that it had reached its limit. It would come no farther and still there was no sign that anything had moved — no opening in the wall.

Dick stepped back a little and he felt his heel catch against something solid and, swinging round, his heart gave a great leap, for directly behind him a large trapdoor had opened. With an exultant cry Palmer released the ring and sprang around to the front and before his very eyes the door, with considerable groaning, descended again. When it had closed there was little to see of its evidence, for the grass had grown on and around the trapdoor, concealing it most effectively.

Cursing, Palmer ran back to the ring and pulled hard on it again, and over his shoulder he saw the trapdoor slowly open. He glanced across at Wild Willie, and the youth still remained silent where he was, watching and grinning eternally. Frantically Palmer looked about for some means of holding the ring, and stretching back at arms-length he glanced over the top of the door. There he saw what he sought: a length of chain with a hook at the end hanging down the inner side of the door. Quickly he pulled this up and attached the hook to the ring. Then he stepped round to the opening again and gazed down into the black pit which was revealed.

Stone steps led down into the blackness and disappeared, and as Dick Palmer stood there, there arose from the pit the faint sound of men's voices and coarse laughter, and Palmer knew then that he was at last upon the verge of discovering the secret of Toby-Joy.

17

Dick Palmer turned to see whether Wild Willie had heard the raucous laughter emanating from the pit, but the youth gave no indication of his thoughts, just standing and smiling in his insane manner. Suddenly he swung round and, with a cackle of laughter, skipped off across the grass and disappeared beyond the ruined walls of the monastery.

When his weird figure with its long black coat had gone Palmer suddenly felt a strange loneliness, but the thought of Jeanette gave him courage and provided the necessary incentive for him to enter the forbidding black pit. The first thing to do was to construct a makeshift torch, for it would prove useless to enter the opening without a light. He could kindle the torch with the tinderbox he always carried with him.

He began looking for suitable brush-wood in which he might hide, now moving quickly, for further unpleasant sounds had reached him from the open trapdoor, and he knew that he could not afford to waste time. Palmer was occupied thus on the slope of the knoll outside the monastery walls when a strange glow was cast upon the ground about him. Abruptly there came a cackle of laughter and spinning round he beheld the grinning Willie standing above him, and in one hand the youth carried a lighted lantern.

'Now, pal,' cried Dick, delighted, 'that's mighty thoughtful of you,' and he scrambled up the slope and gently took the lantern from the wild youth. Willie gave out another laugh and danced off down the knoll and soon had vanished into the wood.

Palmer retraced his steps to the trapdoor, and upon reaching it he lay on his stomach and lowered the lantern down into the pit as far as possible. All that was revealed were more stone steps leading down into the blackness at a steep angle between damp walls of rock. Dick got to his feet again and, taking a deep breath, commenced the descent into the pit.

There were about twenty steps and each one covered in slime, so that Dick had to hold the lantern low down to enable him to take a secure foothold. He reached the bottom and peered ahead along the low, narrow passage that sloped away gently before him. Taking a last glance up at the square of grey sky above, Palmer plunged forward into the repellent passage, pistol in one hand, lantern in the other.

Due to the narrowness of the passage Dick had only to fear what lay ahead or behind. His footsteps echoed eerily as he walked, though he stepped as lightly as he could, and he felt very isolated with just the feeble glow of the lantern as company. But now quite clearly there came to his ears from out of the blackness ahead the sound of rough voices punctuated by an occasional loud guffaw, and in the background was the noise of great bustle and activity.

The former highwayman continued on his way and then all at once he came to a fork in the passage. One way led straight on and the other off to his right. Here he stopped and listened to the voices in the distance, and it was quite clear that the sounds came from the passage that led straight forward. He continued ahead resolutely and the noises grew louder, and Palmer cocked his gun and advanced tight-lipped.

He reached a corner in the passage and realised that beyond was the source of the loud cries and shouts that now vibrated in the dim confines of the passage. Palmer deposited his lantern on the floor Slowly he leaned forward and gazed round the corner. A few paces ahead the passage entered a great, high-ceilinged cellar but Palmer could not see very clearly into this room, for across the exit of the passage was fitted a massive iron portcullis.

The room beyond, as far as Palmer could see from his position, contained a long wide table around which were seated divers numbers of men, and on the tables and in many sconces ranged around the great stone walls were flickering candles throwing a waving, eerie light upon the scene. More details Dick could not make out for it seemed that there were some things attached to the inside of the portcullis that further impeded his view. Leaving his lantern where it was, Dick advanced towards the massive gate, confident of the shelter afforded him by the darkness of the passage. As he neared the portcullis he realised that the 'things' attached to it were, in fact, three human bodies securely tied to the cross members.

Palmer reached the gate and peered through at the three men tied there by their wrists and ankles. And with a gasp of horror he recognised his three friends, Will, Jonathan and Jeremy. His gasp of horror soon changed, however, to a sigh of relief, for he saw that their eyes were open and that they were grimly watching the proceedings taking place in the spacious cellar.

Dick Palmer had now a clear view of the cellar and he noted the fine golden sconces on the walls and on the table — smugglers' trophies without a doubt. Down the great table was piled a fine variety of fruit and vegetables, cold roast chicken, large pieces of venison, beef, pork and lamb on huge decorated plates, and countless numbers of bottles of wine and spirits. Over by one wall stood three barrels of ale. Palmer saw all this and then he surveyed the revellers, of which there were nearly a score, and many were in various stages of drunkenness.

He espied a young woman arguing with one drunken fellow. Some distance along the table was a little fellow with a large, ungainly head, and Dick stared at this man for several moments, for he knew that he had seen him somewhere before. Then he remembered: it was Nodding Ned, the sleepy man in the Grasshopper Inn, where Will and Dick had spent their first night in Surrey. Palmer was aware now who it was that murdered Alfred Lackton, the landlord.

Suddenly Palmer's attention was caught by a plump woman who sat at the head of the table. She wore a highly ornamental, white hair-do and beneath her face was heavily powdered and painted, and adorning her left cheek was a brown patch after the fashion of the day. Recognition came slowly to Dick Palmer, for at first he could hardly believe his eyes; then, with emotional dismay, he knew the identity of 'the Lady' — now at last he understood why she sought with such ardour Will Snell and himself.

It was Charlotte Penfield. Her husband's plan for the control of the Martilliére fortune, rightfully the property of Jeanette, Palmer's wife, had been completely foiled by Dick and Will. Penfield had paid for his wicked scheming with his life.

Charlotte Penfield! A feeling of nausea swept over Dick as it was abruptly borne in upon him that Jeanette was in this evil woman's hands. Palmer had been well aware of Charlotte's maniacal devotion to her husband, and Jeannette had been directly concerned in his death. Palmer felt a cold shiver run through him.

Near her sat Simon Pendexter in deep conversation with Charlotte. It seemed to Dick Palmer that it had taken him hours to inspect this scene but in reality it was but a few seconds.

He glanced up at his three friends tied to the bars of the portcullis. As yet they had not noticed his presence. Dick saw their weary, cut faces, but he noticed, too, that their eyes still sparkled with stubborn optimism in the hope that even now they might escape their terrible fate. Palmer stood on his toes and gently whispered:

'Will!'

The giant's eyes popped wide open and then a great beam of pleasure spread across his red face even before he turned, then he slowly glanced down through the bars, grinning away with delight and heartfelt relief.

'Nay, Dick, but you've been a mighty long time!'

Immediately Jonathan and Jeremy twisted round and they, too, smiled like Cheshire cats at sight of Dick Palmer.

'Look at the front you fools,' muttered Palmer quickly, 'else you'll be seen.'

They did as he ordered, like three obedient boys such was their immeasurable relief at realising that now perhaps there might be a faint chance of effecting their escape. At least they had more reason for hope, and it was noticeable that their bodies straightened in their bonds and a new light entered their eyes. Already Will Snell was cudgeling his brains for some scheme for escape.

'We must wait awhile 'till the swine are more drunken,' he announced.

'Yes, but where's Jeanette and Miss Mathering?' hissed Dick.

'They're waiting until they start messing about with us and then they'll bring them out to watch,' Will replied.

Suddenly Charlotte Penfield stood up, swaying unsteadily, glass clutched in one hand, the other hand gripping the edge of the table. She glared down at the motley company, her small eyes glittering angrily out of her white, painted face.

'Now my fine friends,' cried she, 'where's Dick Palmer?'

'Me lady, me lady,' cried one big ruffian halfway down the big table. 'I 'ave told you the truth — 'e followed us and I think the guards should bring 'im in any moment now.'

Charlotte sat down again with a bump, her multi-coloured petticoats spreading out around her, and tempestuously she inspected the mask that was her face in a large hand-mirror she picked up from the table. With a mutter she replaced the hand-mirror and impatiently drained her glass of gin, then with heaving bosom she stared in exasperation at Pendexter.

'We must act quickly,' whispered Palmer. 'God knows what that woman will do.'

'Listen,' said Will, 'this is our best plan. We must attack 'em from both sides; in fact, we have no alternative as I don't know how to work this damn gate. Cut us down, Dick, and then go back to the Monastery Inn. There is a horse's tail hanging from the fireplace in the taproom. Pull it and the fireplace will open.'

'There's two guards inside,' warned Stark.

'Yes,' said Will. 'You will have to take care of them, Dick. Then when we see you at the opening of that passage yonder we'll attack. By that time the rats should be in a fine state of drunkenness.'

'But Pendexter will see we're free,'

whispered Jeremy out of the corner of his mouth.

'No he won't — not in this dim light. We'll still hang here, but by grasping the bars with our hands.'

'It's a good idea, Will,' said Palmer, 'hold on, then, and I will cut these thongs.'

As Dick Palmer released his friends Charlotte Penfield suddenly jumped to her feet again and cried out in a wild, high-pitched voice: 'Bring in the two women. Let them see what we do to their men.'

Dick Palmer stopped cutting the ropes and stood as if petrified, gazing upon the drunken orgy before him. In a moment two men dragged in Jeanette and Crimson Mathering, who struggled vainly in their grasp. Palmer gave an inarticulate cry at sight of his wife, and Jeremy cursed beneath his breath. Feverishly Palmer cut the remaining ropes.

'You had better be quick, Dick,' grunted Will. 'Don't worry if matters get out of hand; we'll attack without you.'

'Here, then,' whispered Palmer urgently,

'take these three pistols — I have one myself.' He pushed a pistol into each pair of hands.

'Farewell,' Dick murmured, and he turned and hurried back along the passage. Reaching the corner he picked up the lantern and ran as swiftly as he could along the passage. His footsteps echoed eerily about him, tending to make him run ever faster, and a panicky fear clutched hold of him, for he knew that Jeanette's life now depended on how long it would take him to reach the Monastery Inn.

Dick soon came to the stone steps and these he bounded up two at a time. Reaching the top he set off down the slope and away from the monastery. He had not gone far when he decided to discard Wild Willie's lantern, for it encumbered him. Now Palmer ran like a deer through the night, swerving in and out of the trees. Once he fell headlong over a bush but he was upon his feet again at once and on his way. It seemed ages to him before he saw through the trees the dark mass of the Monastery Inn.

Reaching the rear of the house he crept forward between the outhouses and approached the kitchen door. It stood open and he stepped inside and then halted and listened. All appeared to be still and quiet. Suddenly Dick jumped almost two feet into the air as a loud sound broke the silence, then he smiled to himself when he recognised the hoot of an owl from a nearby tree He must calm down else he would fail in his mission and be carried into the monastery cellar as dead as was Alfred Lackton in the bar of the Grasshopper Inn.

In the taproom Palmer eyed the horse's tail hanging from one side of the stone fireplace. He glanced about carefully, scrutinising every dark nook and cranny, to make sure the room was quite empty, then he crossed over to the fireplace and pulled hard on the horse's tail. Immediately there was a heavy creaking and grinding noise and the inner part of the fireplace slowly swung back to reveal a dark hole.

18

Dick Palmer drew his pistol and stepped to one side and waited, watching the large gap at the back of the fireplace. For some time there was not a single sound, but Dick was cool and collected now and he remained out of sight awaiting patiently some movement by the two guards. A clock on the mantelpiece ticked loudly in the silent taproom and every tick seemed to Palmer to be like the blows of the hammer sealing Jeanette's coffin. He gritted his teeth, however, and refrained from leaping forward, entering the tunnel and charging into the monastery cellar. Such an impulsive act he knew would end swiftly in his own demise.

Suddenly there came from the black opening a faint stirring, then there followed a whisper of voices, and Dick Palmer grinned triumphantly and cocked his pistol. Again there was silence and still Palmer watched the gap from his hidden position. A moment later a head appeared and then another, and the two heads glanced apprehensively around the dark taproom.

'Some cove must have opened it, Pete,' said one head. The other nodded: 'Yes, Shorty, but who? There's no one about.'

This statement was digested by the two men, who seemed not at all inclined to step out into the moonlit taproom. Dick Palmer cursed beneath his breath. Would they never come out into the open?

'I fancy we should close it again, Pete, and tell 'em what happened in Toby-Joy.'

'Ha, no, Shorty, you know 'ow the Lady 'ates to be disturbed during 'er entertainment, an' I don't wish to taste the spiked boy.'

'Come on then, don't be a coward; let's step out together.'

Having agreed to this move the two men, each one trying to be last out, slowly crept forward into the taproom, pistols levelled and all of a quiver. Palmer waited until they were in the middle of the room glancing affrightedly about before he went into action. Then he ran softly up behind them, intending to knock them unconscious with the butt of his pistol, but they heard him and swung about with cries of fear.

Palmer discharged his pistol and one of the men crumpled to the floor. The other returned his fire and Dick felt the bullet tug at his sleeve, then he leaped upon the fellow. His antagonist was short and wiry and in the faint light he saw that the rogue had somehow produced a great curved knife. Quickly Palmer drew his own and thus they fought, each one trying to drive home the fatal blow. They swayed back and forth across the floor like dancers, locked together, and in a little while Dick found that his adversary was weakening. His knife drew nearer to the fellow's chest, then with a last great effort he plunged in the blade and the man's choking scream made the blood run cold in Dick Palmer's veins.

He stared down with horror at the squirming body and watched Shorty's contortions slowly grow weaker until, after an interminable time it seemed, he lay still, his eyes glassy and staring.

Palmer shook himself and turned away, breathing heavily and feeling a great revulsion within him, for it was the first time he had killed a man with a knife.

He sat down on a chair to collect himself, then the thought of his wife made him jump to his feet again, and as he did so he heard the sound of running feet in the tunnel behind the fireplace. Realising that it was now of no purpose remaining in the taproom he rushed to the entrance and stepped into the blackness. The footsteps were still a long way away, though they echoed loudly, and Palmer, when his eyes had become used to the dark, made as swift a progress as he could.

He was not sure of his plan now; all he knew was that he must reach the cellar as soon as possible. Abruptly he saw a swinging lantern, a spot of light, far ahead and below him, and at the same time Dick realised that he had not reloaded his pistol. Hastily he withdrew it from his pocket and with feverish fingers began to reload. The lantern appeared not twenty paces away and the outline of a man was now visible. But with a sigh of relief Dick cocked his pistol and was ready.

Grimly he levelled it at the approaching figure running up the slope of the tunnel towards him and clearly seen in the yellow glow of the lantern. Dick was about to squeeze the trigger when he felt a stunning blow upon the back of his head and the lantern seemed to rise and then fade away. He realised he had been cleverly tricked and after that he dropped into a coma and was faintly aware of two men bending over him and saying in gleeful voices things he could not understand.

He felt himself lifted in rough hands and carried down the tunnel. They went on through the engulfing blackness for, it appeared, hours on end. All the time he could faintly hear the hum of voices, punctuated now and then by an evil laugh. Perhaps it was as well, thought Palmer, for now he would be going to the same place as Jeanette and they would be together for ever. But what if he did not go to the same place as her — now he had killed a man with a knife? This thought revolved maddeningly in his brain and he was filled with terror. Ah, if he had only clubbed the little fellow in the taproom — now he was going down and down, and Jeanette was going up and up and every moment further away from him.

Abruptly there was a continuous loud noise in his ears and a glow about him and he knew he was nearing his destination. But strangely he felt that Jeanette was not far away from him after all, and he rejoiced and vowed to make the best of things.

Then there came a cry of exultation and this brought Dick Palmer slowly to his senses, and he felt himself laid down upon some hard object. In a moment he realised that he had been brought to Toby-Joy. Now he must open his eyes gradually else they would discover he had regained consciousness.

Suddenly there was a triumphant scream and Charlotte Penfield's cracked, strident voice rang out: 'At last — at last I have him! He's mine, he's mine — to play with as I will!'

Dick Palmer squinted through his

half-closed eyes and saw above a white, powdered face with a red slash of a mouth and deep, lined eyes that betrayed the woman's age. She reminded him of some wild heathen priestess and all at once, though her wicked eyes glittered with triumph, he found her pitifully amusing.

'Now, what's the programme, me Lady?' asked Pendexter, sitting watching Charlotte Penfield with a slight smile playing upon his lips.

'The programme — the programme?' cried Charlotte, sitting down again. 'Ha — it needs some thought. Not for nothing did I plan and scheme to get this man and his giant friend into my hands. It needs a lot of thought!'

Palmer then heard the woman drinking heavily. When she had finished she gave a gasp, stood up and leaned over her captive again. Palmer could feel her breath upon his cheek.

'Bring the girl to me,' Charlotte called, still poised like a vulture above the outstretched form of Dick Palmer. Immediately Dick realised that she meant

Jeanette and as he heard footsteps approaching, one pair of which was dragging over the flagstones of the cellar, he found it hard not to open his eyes. But he knew he must not, that the time to open his eyes was when he began the fight. He knew, too, that his friends on the portcullis must now be waiting for him to give the signal for attack. But no! — they did not know he was conscious! Then he should attack soon, for it was essential that he make the first move and thus draw attention away from his friends.

'Dick!' It was a soft cry of anxiety from Jeanette who now stood by the table, her arms twisted behind her back by Nodding Ned, who was at her side, grinning all over his large face. Palmer sighed with relief at the sound of her voice.

Simon Pendexter suddenly got to his feet and announced: 'Whilst you're planning your own entertainment, my Lady, I think I shall have a little of my own with my pal, Jonathan, over there. Me spiked boy has been thirsting after his sharp nose for a long time.' And though Palmer could not see the great fellow he felt instinctively that Pendexter was twirling about his hand his terrible weapon.

'Bring the fellow up here, Simon,' suggested Charlotte Penfield, 'and let us all watch — you must not be selfish!'

Dick Palmer knew then that now was his time for action, else Pendexter would discover his friends were free and all would be lost.

19

Dick Palmer sprang quickly from the table, sweeping Charlotte Penfield to one side, and Simon Pendexter, before he knew what was happening, suddenly found the 'spiked boy' torn from his grasp and thrown in a far corner. Immediately there was an uproar. Palmer turned upon Nodding Ned, and this worthy swiftly released Jeanette, whipped from his pocket a glittering sailor's knife and met Dick's attack with a fierce lunge.

Palmer ducked and the knife cleaved the air not an inch above his head. He closed in and grappled with the little man and m a moment managed to force the fellow to drop his knife. As they fought Dick saw out of the corner of his eyes, Will Snell, Jonathan Stark and Jeremy Mathering grimly advancing towards the table, their pistols cocked and levelled, waiting until they were near the table before firing so as to ensure their bullets found their mark.

At least twelve ruffians now stood up, staring in bewilderment at the three men walking towards them, and another twelve lay, drunk, in various ungainly postures on each side of the table.

'Wake up, you fools,' screamed Pendexter, 'and at 'em — there's only four.'

At this shout three shots rang out and three men dropped dead: simultaneously one of the young girls grabbed a bottle and smashed it down with all her strength upon the nearest man, and the surprised fellow sank senseless to the floor.

'You little vixen,' cried another, a massive, bearded sailor, and he in turn picked up a bottle and crashed it down with mighty force upon the girl's head, and she fell to the cold floor with a broken scalp. Then Will Snell was upon the rogue and he dealt him a blow that sounded like the crunch of a battering ram against a heavy door.

The battle of Toby-Joy was on! Dick Palmer had disposed of Nodding Ned, with the help of his wife; she had discovered a stick and had beaten the fellow's great head with it until he was senseless. The second girl joined Jeanette, and Palmer recognised her as Mary Lackton. The other girl, who lay dead, was undoubtedly the blacksmith's daughter, Betty Broughton who, like the others, was being held to ransom.

Will Snell, in between his battles with divers numbers of half-drunken men, glanced hither and thither for sight of Crimson Mathering. So did Jeremy, who was engaged in a fierce knife fight with a short, squat fellow who was about half his height. But Crimson Mathering was nowhere to be seen. This was no wonder, for she was beneath the table struggling with the unspeakable Charlotte Penfield. But the 'Lady' was no match for Crimson Mathering.

Simon Pendexter cocked his pistol and took cool, deliberate aim at Jonathan Stark, who was at that moment banging his opponent's head upon the far wall. It was just before Pendexter pulled the trigger that Charlotte Penfield, her hair-do awry, her powdered face patchy and scratched and a wild look in her eyes, tried to escape from Crimson Mathering. She scrambled out from beneath the table and stood up.

At the same time Pendexter squeezed the trigger, but his warning shout was too late, for the shot entered Charlotte's heart. She fell across the table without as much as a gasp, slipped on to the floor and lay still, her fine petticoats sadly dishevelled, her magnificent hair a straggly, forlorn sight. Such was the end of Charlotte Penfield, wife of the Squire of High Beach. She lay upon the floor of her highwayman's hostel amongst the spilt ale and wine like a discarded puppet.

Crimson Mathering crawled out from beneath the table and joined Jeanette and Mary Lackton, and the three women watched, wide-eyed, the bloody battle that was taking place before their eyes.

Simon Pendexter ran up behind Will Snell, at the moment engaged in a fierce tussle with two clumsy seamen, one of whom was completely bald. Pendexter drew his knife and raised it high above his head, and Crimson Mathering screamed with terror and covered her eyes.

Her scream drew Jeremy's attention, still ferociously fighting the fellow half his size, and with a curse the lanky man brought up his knee swiftly and caught his adversary a resounding smack on his unshaven chin. Then Jeremy leaped to the table picked up a bottle and threw it, with a mighty swing of his long arm at Pendexter. The bottle caught the blonde giant a glancing blow before he was able to bury his knife in Will's back, and he staggered away and came to rest against the side of the table.

Will Snell turned quickly and swung his fist at Pendexter and the latter, still particularly dazed, took the blow on his chest, stumbled, and collapsed beneath the table. Will could not pay him any further attention, for he was attacked again by his former opponents. Dick Palmer, on the other side of the table, was in dire straits, for a great one-eyed brute had leaped upon him and was thumping his face with his huge fists. The three women at once jumped upon the fellow and their combined efforts proved most effective for he must needs scramble to his feet and fight them all. Immediately Palmer got painfully to his feet and, using his heavy pistol as a club, brought it down with all his strength upon the back of the fellow's hairy head. The one-eyed smuggler promptly buckled at the knees and joined the ever-increasing number of bodies sprawled, either unconscious or dead, all over the floor of Toby-Joy.

The battle was almost won, it seemed, for only five men, including Pendexter, remained on their feet and they appeared to be swiftly losing any enthusiasm they might have had for further battle. Jonathan Stark, an excited gleam in his dark eyes, his short, black beard jutting out in a most pugnacious fashion, glanced around for further work, but it really seemed there was none! Will Snell was cheerfully banging his opponents' heads together, Jeremy was sitting astride a man in the middle of the table, amongst the choice meats and vegetables; and Dick Palmer was doing battle with no one, but appeared most concerned with a large rent in his breeches.

Suddenly Stark gave a cry: 'Where is he — where's Simon Pendexter?'

At this everybody looked around, but the greatest rogue of all was nowhere to be seen. There was silence, whilst they all had a good look about the cellar, then a scuffle was heard and Pendexter suddenly scrambled out from the far end of the table. Within a moment he was racing for the portcullis at the distant end of the chamber. At once a whoop went up from the four men and, like hounds to the chase, they charged after Simon Pendexter.

Pendexter reached the wall near the portcullis and pulled a concealed lever and, with a great clanking, the gate slowly began to rise. He ducked underneath and disappeared into the dark passage beyond. Shouting like madmen the four friends followed not twenty paces behind.

But they had to slow down for they could not see their hands before their faces in the blackness of the passage. Clearly ahead they could hear Pendexter's echoing footsteps and, with a curse, Stark cried out that they were losing pace. Such was the case for Pendexter obviously knew the windings of the passage better than his pursuers.

Abruptly the four men came upon the fork and here they must needs stop to ascertain which path Pendexter had taken. It was the one to the left, which Dick Palmer did not know, and grimly they followed as best they could. Stark kept up a flow of curses, which rose to a pitch each time he stumbled into a wall. Thus they continued along the passage, knocking and scraping their limbs at every unseen corner. They proceeded two abreast and as a consequence got in each other's way, and their tempers were sorely tried. The four friends were over anxious, fearing that they might now, on the verge of victory, lose the biggest prize of all.

The passage seemed to go on and on, and now with dismay they realised that Simon Pendexter's footsteps were growing fainter. At last, far ahead, they saw a grey glow and were able to traverse the remainder of the passage at increased speed. The glow grew stronger and now they could see that it was a small hole, and the light that penetrated into the passage was that of the moon. As they drew nearer they found the hole of light was some distance above them, and immediately the passage began to slope steeply upwards.

With a gasp of triumph Jonathan Stark scrambled out through the hole and was joined by his three companions, and they found themselves standing in a large thicket to the West and slightly below the ruined monastery. And as they stood there in the light of the moon that shone down out of a fine, star-lit sky, they heard the sound of a horse's hoofs in the wood below.

From their position the four men could see the moonlit road which led North to Slinfold and South to Littlehampton via the Inn by the River. As they watched a single horseman broke out of the trees and at a fast gallop turned south. He had not ridden far when he glanced back over his shoulder and, seeing the four discon- solate men standing in the middle of the thicket, he waved cheerfully and the moon shone on his fair hair. Then he had turned again to his front, spurred his horse to greater efforts and in a moment had vanished along the highway.

Jonathan Stark stood for a long time afterwards staring at the point where Simon Pendexter had passed out of sight, and on his sharp face there was a look that was the embodiment of rage, frustration and dismay.

At last he turned and cheerlessly led the way back to the opening to the passage that had served Simon Pendexter so well as an escape route. The four men scrambled back into the passage and retraced their steps in gloomy silence to the spacious cellar. Coming upon this place they stopped dead at the portcullis and stared aghast upon the scene that lay before them. The cellar appeared as if a tornado had swept through it, leaving in its wake disorder, confusion and bloody death. The feast was scattered willy-nilly about the floor and everywhere lay broken bottles. Amongst this riotous scene stumbled drunken and groaning men, and on the far side the three girls crouched in fear. Realising their folly in leaving the three women alone in the cellar the four men hurried forward — as best they could for they suddenly realised they were all sorely wounded and greatly weary. They escorted the women into the tunnel leading back to the Monastery Inn. At last they came into the taproom and there they sat down to regain their breath and discuss the past events.

'I see by your woebegone expression, Mister Stark,' said Crimson, 'that you failed to apprehend that awful man, Simon Pendexter.'

'Yes, oh dear, yes — I avow it's a mortifying blow.'

Jeanette had crossed to her husband and was inspecting, with some consternation, his divers small wounds. Crimson stepped over to Will Snell and inspected him and then her brother, Jeremy. Seeing that Jonathan Stark was receiving no attention, Mary Lackton timidly approached him and did what she could to relieve his injuries. So the four men sat back and enjoyed themselves, for, if the truth be known, except for their wounds and the disappointment of not capturing Simon Pendexter, they were in quite high spirits.

'Nay, but we sit here in a taproom surrounded by ale and we don't touch a drop,' cried Stark. He promptly rose to his feet and disappeared behind the bar with the obvious intention of rectifying this state of affairs.

'Yes, I'm mighty thirsty,' announced Will Snell. Soon Jonathan reappeared carrying a tray and on the tray were four foaming tankards of ale, at which the other three licked their lips thirstily.

Stark drank his ale with a gloomy countenance, staring at the floor in far distant thought. Dick Palmer noted his friend's forlorn look and cried:

'Come, come, Jonathan, cheer up. After all we have solved the riddle of Toby-Joy. Don't worry, Pendexter will be brought to book. Such a scoundrel cannot remain free for ever.'

'Ha,' grunted Stark, pinching his neat beard, 'you can afford to be optimistic for you don't know him as well as I. It seems the Gods are always on his side, for he escapes me every time — he's like the proverbial cat with the nine lives.'

'Huh,' growled Will, 'if that's so then

he's on his last life, for next time I meet him, as meet him I shall, he will not escape.'

'Now, now, let there be an end to talk of death,' cried Crimson. 'Tonight you have had enough to last you the rest of your days.'

At this moment horses' hooves were heard on the road and they came to a halt outside the inn. Shortly afterwards there was a great knocking upon the door. At once the men crowded into a dark corner while Jeremy Mathering stepped forward and swung open the door.

'We're officers of the law from Bow Street,' cried a deep voice. 'We understand this is the headquarters of the gang of robbers we seek?'

'You understand correctly,' replied Jeremy, pulling wide the door. Four men stepped into the taproom and Will Snell immediately recognised them for the officers he and Dick had encountered when first they rode into Surrey. A big, black-haired fellow with a squint appeared to be the leader and, upon seeing the group in the corner, he growled: 'And who might you be?'

Will strode forward and bowed: 'May I introduce myself — my name is Will Snell.'

'Ha, the man we sought,' cried the peace officer with the squint.

'But the constable at Pulborough holds the real men you seek.'

'That's correct — now where's the rest of this gang?'

Will pointed to the opening at the back of the fireplace. 'Down there,' he replied.

The officer stared unenthusiastically at the black hole. 'An' what's down there?'

'A number of dead men and women!'

'Ho, I see,' said he, and as Palmer and Stark joined Will Snell, the officer noted in the moonlight the bloody appearance of the four men. 'And it seems,' the officer added with quite a pleasant smile, 'that you've all been having a nice little scrap!'

'Yes,' said Jeanette, 'you might call it a 'little scrap.' But I think it was a mighty big one!'

Giving a cordial nod, the officer with the squint carried on across the room followed by his henchmen, and in a moment they had filed into the black opening and disappeared.

Crimson Mathering turned round to her friends. 'Now,' cried she, brushing back a long lock of red hair on her forehead, 'you're all coming back to Mathering Manor to be my guests.'

'Oh, that's kind of you,' exclaimed Jeanette, 'but please don't bother.'

'No bother,' replied Crimson. 'I insist — so come, let us mount and get on our way.'

All of them were glad of the offer, for it meant a good night's sleep — what there was left of the night — instead of a long journey. So the men went out and collected their steeds and in a little while they were mounted, some of the horses with a double load, and subsequently were on the road to Ewhurst and Mathering Manor.

20

The four men spent a week at Mathering Manor recuperating from their fight at Toby-Joy. During this period Dick Palmer and Jeanette often walked in the lovely surrounding countryside, and often on these trips they met two red heads, and often these two were in heated argument. Once they came upon Crimson standing before Will and shaking her tiny fist beneath his red face.

'It's not a game for kids, as you call it, Will Snell — it's a game for grown up people and is the most marvellous thing on this great world of ours!'

Dick Palmer grinned at his wife and he enquired, as they joined their friends: 'What's the most marvellous thing on this great world of ours, Crimson?'

The girl turned heatedly upon Palmer, her face flushed almost the colour of her hair. 'Marriage,' cried she, 'marriage — that's what we are discussing — and that's the most marvellous thing in this great world of ours.' She added: 'He,' with contemptuous emphasis on the word, 'thinks it's for kids!'

'Ha, then I'm a kid,' remarked Palmer with a laugh.

'Of course it's not,' said Jeanette warmly. 'I agree with Crimson — it is the most marvellous thing!'

Will Snell shrugged his mighty shoulders and grinned at Crimson, who glared back at him. 'So be it — let's end it there.'

The four returned to the Manor, Crimson Mathering pouting and silent, but soon she had forgotten the argument and was buzzing about preparing the evening meal for her many guests. She received great help in her duties about the house from Jeanette and Mary Lackton. Mary, in the happy atmosphere of the Manor, was slowly forgetting her terrible experience and the horrible death of her father at the Grasshopper Inn.

It was one evening towards the end of the week that a strange man came riding up to Mathering Manor and, upon being confronted by Bob Flint, asked to speak to Jonathan Stark. That worthy had been asleep in the small lounge and, upon hearing the voices outside, he came running out, smoothing his short beard, his eyes alight with excitement

'Well, Tom Fagg, what news have you?'

'He is taken, Mister Stark — the catchpolls caught him near Shamley Green. They're this moment on their way to London and Newgate jail.'

Jonathan Stark muttered a curse and stared thoughtfully down at his feet. At last he looked up: 'Thank you, Tom, your work is done. I must go myself now to London.'

The man Fagg touched his cap in salute and then wheeled his horse about and galloped away down the drive. Stark turned and walked back into the house and so deep in thought was he that he nearly bumped into Will Snell who was on his way out.

'Now, pal, what's up?' asked Will.

Stark glanced up at the red-headed giant and appeared to be considering whether to confide in him or not, He decided to do so, for he replied: 'This many a day, Will I have been seeking a certain man — a gentleman o' the road called Jack Cambridge — as has my fine friend Pendexter. Cambridge holds a chart, which I know leads the way to unbelievable wealth. At all costs must I get it: before Pendexter, but now I hear Cambridge has been apprehended and taken to Newgate — and that, as you know, means Tyburn gallows.'

'What do you intend next, then?'

'I don't know, but to London I must go — maybe there, somehow, I can procure the chart.'

Jonathan Stark studied the giant standing before him and he pinched his black beard in a thoughtful manner. 'You know, Will, I'm alone on this little venture, but I have sworn to obtain the chart before Pendexter. If he interferes, which I know he will, then it may be my chance to repay him for murdering my sister. Now then, a fellow such as you on my side would be a mighty good thing. How about joining me?'

Will Snell's deep blue eyes gleamed and he lightly touched the small scar that ran across his temple, the work of Simon Pendexter on the road to Toby-Joy.

'It's a fine idea, Jonathan, I'll certainly join you in your venture.'

Stark delightedly shook the great paw that was proffered him. 'I avow we shall make a resourceful pair, Will. We shall ride tomorrow and we can accompany Dick and his wife, for they leave for their home tomorrow.'

At this moment there were quick footsteps in the passage and Crimson Mathering appeared. She stopped abruptly and stared at the two men. 'An' what are you two villains up to?'

Will Snell looked embarrassed, which made him appear most awkward and clumsy, but Jonathan Stark replied: 'Why it's just that Will and I have decided to accompany Dick and Jeanette to London tomorrow.'

Crimson Mathering's green eyes swept round upon Will Snell and she stared up at him for several moments, the while the giant looked this way and that and acted most sheepish. Then, without a word, Crimson stormed past them. When she had passed out of sight her usual exuberance appeared to evaporate and, finding a seat in the garden, she sat down heavily and stared down at the ground in dismay.

Upon the morrow the horses were saddled and Jeanette went over to Crimson, standing in the porch, and kissed her goodbye and at the same time whispered something in her ear. Crimson smiled slightly and nodded and set her red lips in a determined line.

Then Dick Palmer assisted his wife into the saddle and all four were ready for the road. With a final wave they dug in their spurs and went cantering down the drive of Mathering Manor. The mistress of the house for a moment stood sadly gazing after them and her eyes were for one person only. Will turned again, just before he passed through the gate, and waved for the second time, but he was too late; Crimson Mathering had already run quickly back into the house.

So Dick Palmer and his beautiful wife returned to their home on the outskirts of London, and Jonathan Stark and Will Snell set off on a new adventure, which is another story altogether.

THE END

We do hope that you have enjoyed reading this large print book.

Did you know that all of our titles are available for purchase?

We publish a wide range of high quality large print books including:
Romances, Mysteries, Classics
General Fiction
Non Fiction and Westerns

Special interest titles available in large print are:
The Little Oxford Dictionary
Music Book, Song Book
Hymn Book, Service Book

Also available from us courtesy of Oxford University Press:
Young Readers' Dictionary
(large print edition)
Young Readers' Thesaurus
(large print edition)

For further information or a free brochure, please contact us at:
Ulverscroft Large Print Books Ltd.,
The Green, Bradgate Road, Anstey,
Leicester, LE7 7FU, England.
Tel: (00 44) **0116 236 4325**
Fax: (00 44) **0116 234 0205**

Other titles in the
Linford Mystery Library:

RICOCHET

J. F. Straker

John Everard is a cold, ruthless businessman. When he returns home from a business trip he discovers that his Spanish wife Juanita and baby son Tommy have disappeared, his house has been burgled, and his firm's payroll stolen. Moreover, it was his wife who was seen driving the thieves away in Everard's own Jaguar. Has Juanita been kidnapped — or is she implicated in the robbery? And where is Tommy? Now, with little police co-operation, Everard begins his own investigation . . .

FOOL'S PARADISE

John Russell Fearn

In a fit of pique, Milly Morton — confidential 'secretary' to industrialist Mortimer Bland — deliberately smashed the astronomical plates of Bland's Chief Scientist, Anton Drew. Furthermore, she'd destroyed data which would warn the world of a forthcoming cosmic disaster. The unprecedented violent storms, signs of approaching doom, went unrecognized. Eventually Drew, aided by his friends Ken and Thayleen West, convinced the Prime Minister of the danger — but would it be too late to save the world?

DEATH COMES CALLING

John Glasby

In Los Angeles, the wealthy Marcia Edwards asks investigator Johnny Merak to find her missing grandson. Merak suspects it's a mob kidnapping. There's someone else who wants to hire him: the model Angela Cliveden, who has been receiving life-threatening phone calls. Merak discovers that she is the girlfriend of Tony Minello of the local Mafia. But when she is found murdered in her apartment, Merak is trapped in a potential Mob War and matching his wits with a cunning serial killer.

DEVIL'S PEAK

Brian Ball

Stranded in a High Peak transport café during a freak snowstorm, Jerry Howard finds himself in a vortex of Satanism. Brenda was a motorway girl with a strange scar on her back. The Mark of the Beast. She knew the history of the Brindley legend. And she alone knew the rites. She had been on Devil's Peak before. Now it was Walpurgisnacht and the horned goat was expected. Events moved to a horrendous climax . . .

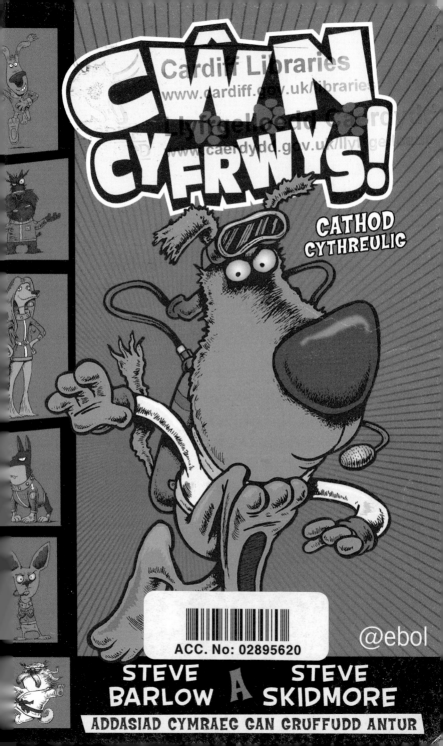

Y fersiwn Cymraeg:
© Atebol Cyfyngedig, Adeiladau'r Fagwyr,
Llanfihangel Genau'r Glyn, Aberystwyth, Ceredigion SY24 5AQ

Cyhoeddwyd gan Atebol Cyfyngedig yn 2013. Cedwir pob hawl.

Addaswyd gan Gruffudd Antur

Dyluniwyd gan Owain Hammonds

Golygwyd gan Adran Olygyddol Cyngor Llyfrau Cymru

Cyhoeddwyd gyda chymorth ariannol Cyngor Llyfrau Cymru

Argraffwyd gan Wasg Cambria, Aberystwyth

www.atebol.com